BEING T

The Early Years

I f you are a first timer to the *Being There* Family, I urge you to read the exciting prequel to **Being There Discovery, Being There Awakenings**. You will maximize your enjoyment of the series by familiarizing yourself with the characters and the history that follows Christian, as well as his friends and family.

In addition, you will get to meet the first fans to be immortalized in print, brothers Chris and Connor from New York. They are the first recipients to become characters in the **Being There Series...The Original Fan Interactive Series**.

Will you be the next character in the series?

Please remember, 'Fan Interactive' means your participation in this, the Original *Being There* Interactive Series, is important to bringing you what you like to read in the series. In order to continue to bring you exciting new adventures in the *Being There* Series, your opinion and suggestions are important, so please visit Amazon.com to share your experience with the world. Five Star reviews are best, but please be honest in your rating.

Please visit https://www.facebook.com/rchenningsenofficial/ to post your comments, or you may send those comments to rc@rchenningsen.com and I will post them for you.

Join in the fun and submit your vote and/or suggestions in our **Interactive Character Search** at **www.BeingThereDiscovery.com** and vote for your favorite ending or submit your suggestion for your chance to be immortalized in print. You may be the next character added to the series, and remember my friends...

Life is best when we participate; live it with passion!

RC

HERE'S WHAT FANS ARE SAYING

ABOUT BOOK ONE
OF THE *BEING THERE* SERIES
OF INTERACTIVE NOVELS.

"From the beginning I was totally captivated and immersed in Christian's journey of a lifetime as the character discovered his abilities. Living a life on the run and trying to hide his abilities was fun. For me it is a captivating novel with suspense, sadness and at the same time excitement. Just love it!"

Amazon Customer

"It was a wonderful book and I thoroughly enjoyed it. The story rotates around the main and strong character, Christian. This is an action packed science fiction genre plot and the author has done a good job by writing an impressive story with interesting characters. I love to read these kinds of fiction story books more and more."

Zoe T. – Kindle Reader

"Easy and most enjoyable read – finished in a couple of sittings. Descriptive writing allows the imagination to run but really, this would make an even better movie – captivating story with lots of room for Hollywood effects."

Doug – Amazon Customer

"I absolutely loved this book. I couldn't wait to see what happens next to Christian. I haven't read a page turner like this in a long time. It was great to be able to lose myself in this exciting novel. I look forward to reading about Christian's new adventures."

Rose Ann S., Long Island, New York

Editor: Nita Robinson
Nita Helping Hand?
www.NitaHelpingHand.com

Cover Design: Jessica James *Pro_Designx*

Layout: Anne Karklins
annekarklins@gmail.com

ISBN-13: 978-1-988071-32-9
ISBN-10: 1988071321

Being There

There

DISCOVERY

The Early Years

R.C. Henningsen

DEDICATION

Being There Discovery... The Early Years is dedicated to the members and fans of the Being There Series of novels. It is through your sharing, generosity and kind words that the debut novel in the series, Being There Awakenings reached International Best Seller Status in less than twenty-four hours. I am humbled by your response and honored to share in the creative process with each of you. Together we will continue to create a series of novels like no other.

NOTE FROM THE AUTHOR

I'd like to personally thank and welcome you to the *Being There* Family of Interactive Novels... The Original fan interactive series where you and readers just like you participate in the development of the series and have an opportunity to become a character in this exciting new series. Imagine... your name as a character, immortalized in print for the world to see in the most exciting new series to hit the shelf in years. To learn more on how to join the *Being There* Insiders Team, please visit www.rchenningsenauthor.com/ Fan-Interactive tab.

I realize your time is important to you, and it is important to me as well. That's why I have dedicated myself to bringing you the most enjoyable, action-packed, emotionally charged Sci-fi action adventures possible.

No matter what genre you read, you will be thrilled and entertained as you are drawn into the storyline, sharing the emotionally charged adventures with the characters. Your heart will pound and your palms may sweat as you are pulled into the action, thrills and excitement of this inventive world created. So get ready... grab a snack and a seat and enjoy The *Being There* Series of novels.

ACKNOWLEDGEMENTS

Being There Discovery... The Early Years could not have been written without the support and talents of many people, and for each of them I am truly grateful. Much like the debut of the series, Being There Awakenings, the team behind Being There Discovery... The Early Years has gone above and beyond in their efforts to bring you the continuation of this International Best Selling Interactive series:

To Peggy McColl, a friend and mentor who was instrumental from the onset of the series – thank you for sharing your inspiration, support and guidance.

To Judy O'Beirn, President and Founder of Hasmark Publishing. Thank you for your insight in assembling the perfect team to bring the Being There Series of Novels to the next level. I am grateful for your focus and professionalism.

To Jenn Gibson, thank you for your advice and efforts in coordinating each and every task in the production of the series. Your actions and resourcefulness are truly appreciated.

To Nita Robinson, Ginger Marks, Anne Karklins. Thank you for sharing your expertise, opinions, and critiques. I am grateful for your willingness to fit a complete review of the Being There novels into your tight schedules.

To Henryez, Khaled and Marlene... the team of artists and creators. I am grateful for your talents in creating the cover images and sketches from simple descriptions. Thank you for sharing your talents.

To Jessica James from Pro_designx, thank you for your ability to turn art into covers. I truly appreciate your sincerity and professionalism.

Thank you all for your efforts, talents and professionalism.

TABLE OF CONTENTS

– One –
The Smell of Freedom

Channarong sprang up from the creaky old cot, startling Christian, and swatted him on the leg. "C'mon it's time to get out of here. It'll be light out soon," he urged in a hurried tone as he walked to the heavy steel door that had separated Christian from the outside world for nearly two months.

The two had been chatting for the better part of an hour. Christian's primary focus was to learn all that he could about Amy and her condition following the dreadful events of that night. So intense was his focus that he hadn't even thought to ask how and why CB, short for Channarong, was there.

"Follow me," CB grunted, pushing hard to open the door.

Christian's face filled with curiosity, "How'd you do that?"

CB jingled the keys to the door wearing the telltale smirk that often accompanies his infrequent ruses.

"Are you freaking kidding me?" Christian barked, muffling his voice so as not to be heard by the guards. "You mean I could have been out of here an hour ago?"

"I thought you liked it here," CB responded with a playful tone as he walked through the doorway, smirking.

Christian huffed, following close behind.

With keen eyes and ears CB led Christian slowly toward the first door in the maze of doors and stairwells that would lead them to freedom. His nerves tightly wound, Christian asked, "How do you expect us to get out of here? You don't think we can just walk out, do you?"

"I have my tricks! C'mon, hurry up," CB confidently smiled.

Christian's pulse raced as they peered through each door and around every corner, waiting to come face to face with his captors. Every step forward was one step closer to freeing him from the nearly two months of solitude he had endured as a guest of this secretive government organization.

He anxiously grabbed CB's arm. "The first guard post is just around the corner... be careful!" A single bead of sweat rolled down the side of his face.

"Don't worry, I've got this," CB assured him.

Christian, unaware that his friend had used an ancient Chinese technique to render the guards unconscious, watched intently as his friend, with the stealth of a big cat hunting its prey, edged his way closer to the guard sitting quietly at his post. "What the hell are you doing?" Christian mumbled under his breath. CB turned and with his finger across his lips, shushed him.

Sly and steady he reached for the guard from behind, pausing for a moment before lunging forward and quickly pulling a small needle from the back of the guard's neck. He spun around in a flash with that damned grin on his face and showed the silk-bound needle to his jumpy friend.

"Pheeeew!" Christian sighed, his unsettled face relaxing as he shook his head in disbelief at the continued antics of his friend. "What the hell was all that sneaking up stuff for? I'm about ready to jump out of my skin for god's sake," Christian bitched in a suppressed tone.

"I told you I had it covered," CB winked.

"Stop screwing around, my freaking heart is pounding. C'mon let's get out of here," Christian implored.

CB led the way, hastening his pace to appease his jittery friend. The pair made their way past four more guard posts, stopping at each to remove a carefully placed pin from each guard's neck.

CB's timing was not happenstance, nor was his casual demeanor. He was this way in just about any situation, good or bad... it's just the way he was. After a month and a half of trying to find Christian's whereabouts, he carefully studied the activity around the building for the better part of two weeks waiting for the right opportunity to employ his plan.

The unassuming building adjacent to Langley Airforce Base was home base for the unnamed secretive organization unofficially tagged the God Hunters by the agents under the watchful eyes of Pamela Kearns. Other than hosting the occasional incarcerate, it housed a few executive level agents as well as handful of scientists and technicians that worked one of two shifts, leaving the facility mostly unoccupied and lightly guarded during the darkness of late night and early morning hours.

With freedom in sight they reached the last guard and pulled the pin from his chubby neck. Christian peered out of the front entrance. His excitement grew knowing he was moments away from seeing the outside world for the first time since he relinquished his freedom to the tenacious Pamela Kearns. Kearns is an over-assertive agent who gained her title through the elimination of her mentor Dr. Stedwell. Stedwell, along with Christian's father, had helped to protect a young Christian from a lifetime of government experimentation.

"I still can't believe you sat in my cell talking to me for almost an hour, you dopey son of a bitch," Christian said in a semi jocular tone and shoving CB.

"Hey, the door was open... " CB defended lightly.

Christian usually appreciated CB's carefree attitude, but this time was different. With the exception of the time spent inside his own mind and memories, he hadn't seen anything outside of his cell for longer than he wished to remember, but still he couldn't help but wonder why CB always took things so nonchalantly. Forgetting his ability to connect telepathically, Christian wondered, "What is it about him? For as many life-times as I can remember and even under the most dangerous circumstances, situations that would fill the average man with fear or his shorts with something else, he just seems to coast through it all as if he hadn't a care in the world..."

"I'll tell you later... Now's not the time," CB abruptly interrupted.

"You heard that?" Christian's face flushed, not realizing he was still connected.

CB approached the entranceway and cautiously scanned for activity outside. "Hurry up! You walk like you drive," he said as he pushed the door open.

"That smells great!" Christian inhaled deeply as a rush of cold morning air passed through the door.

"Really? We're next to the airport sewage treatment facility and that smells great to you?" CB looked at him strangely. Christian smiled without response – he was free.

"Where to?" Christian asked, shrouding his eyes from the parking lot lights glaring in the early morning darkness.

"The car's over here. Got one I think you'll like." CB pointed to a familiar shape off in the distance.

"Nice!" Christian applauded, smiling as he approached the recognizable silhouette, a brand new Mustang GT. Opening the door he took a quick glance in the back seat.

"What are you looking for?" CB questioned, with an inquisitive look.

"You're kidding right?" Christian's eyes hopped from the back seat to CB. "Just making sure we didn't have a passenger like when you picked me up from the airport," he said climbing into the front seat.

CB cranked up the throaty GT and headed for the exit, making one more stop before exiting the facility. Christian watched as he hopped out at the guard booth to remove the final pin from the slumped over guard's neck.

"I've really got to remember that trick," he mumbled admiringly.

CB propped the guard up in his chair, patted him gently on the head and returned to the car to put some distance between them and the agency.

Exiting the facility, Christian once again turned his thoughts to Amy and the nightmare of New Year's Eve.

"I know you're going to think this is crazy, but I have to see her." He paused, reflecting on that fateful night and glanced at CB with a look of determination. "I have to – it's my fault she's where she is. I can't get that night out of my mind – I remember how I held her in my arms, both of us covered in her blood. I've never seen so much blood... You know I have to see her."

"No problem, we'll make it happen," CB sighed with concern, retiring his playful side for the moment, knowing there was no way to dissuade him from his decision, regardless of the danger involved.

The decision made, Christian continued to question CB about all that had transpired since that New Year's Eve and, as in his cell, he focused his inquiry mainly on Amy. CB answered honestly while driving to the small community where he had "borrowed" the Mustang.

Christian's face was a screenplay of emotions as CB answered each of his questions in detail. He explained the harassment his family and friends were subjected to at the hands of Pamela Kearns and her subordinates following New Year's Eve. At Christian's request, he again shared the painful details of Amy's condition and all that had been done to save her life.

"Thank you for being straight with me," he mumbled in a low tone, his face straining with self-imposed pain and guilt, and fell sadly silent.

CB reflected on their past together. Christian had always worn his heart on his sleeve through as many lifetimes as he could remember. He always held family and friends dear and fell in love at the drop of a hat. He smiled fondly, remembering more pleasant times past.

He again realized that that's what made them such a good pair through the many lifetimes they had shared over the millennia. His carefree and uninhibited approach when it came to dangerous situations or challenges, and Christian's emotional strength acting as the voice of reason – sometimes, but this was not one of those times. This time Christian was acting from a place of guilt without reasoning and this concerned CB.

Turning the GT down a quiet tree-lined street, he switched off the headlights and pulled in behind an old silver pickup truck just as dawn started to break.

"Here – change into these, they'll look a lot better than those prison scrubs. We'll be taking that truck." He handed Christian a small duffle bag from the back seat and pointed to the silver pickup.

"I'll be back in a minute, there's one more thing I have to take care of." CB hopped out of the car and hustled his way across the street. Christian watched curiously as he disappeared into the darkness, making his way up a long, narrow driveway.

"Damn, it's cold out here." Christian shivered from the winter's morning air. He jumped into the pickup to change into civilian attire.

What in god's name is that smell?" he mumbled, fumbling to dress himself. His nostrils flared from the increasingly pungent odor.

Moments later CB emerged from the driveway. Scanning the surroundings carefully he sprinted across the street to the pickup and climbed into the driver's seat.

"What was that about?" Christian asked.

"I just had to wake up my new friend. After all, whether he knows it or not, he did lend me his car," CB said with a smirk, tapping his wristband that held a multitude of silk wrapped needles. "Where to first?"

Christian turned to him with the look of unyielding determination.

"That's what I thought," CB replied with a halfhearted smile, "You always did like a challenge." CB kicked over the truck and put it into gear, leaving the quiet neighborhood and his "new friend" to the action that would soon unfold at the hands of Pamela Kearns' investigative team. Chilled from his wardrobe change, Christian flipped on the heat.

"Oh, god!" he gagged, coughing and swatting at a plume of vent dust. "What the hell is that?"

Not sparing CB, the pungent cloud of moldy dust enveloped his face with a vengeance, coating his throat and eyes.

"Son of a bitch!" He coughed as the putrid plume choked him. "It feels like I have sawdust in my eyes," he complained, fumbling to roll down the old truck window.

"Where the hell did you get this nasty thing?" Christian asked as he covered his mouth and nose with his prison scrubs. His face wretched from the god-awful odor as he too fumbled to get the old crank-style window down for some well needed fresh air.

"Farmhouse," cough "just up the road," cough. CB choked out in a coarse voice. In the darkness of night CB didn't realize that he had swiped a truck used for moving fertilizer.

The air finally cleared, but the smell lingered as the putrid smelling dust lining the inside of their nostrils provided them with an ample reminder of the event.

"Where are you going, wasn't that the parkway entrance?" Christian's antenna went up as CB passed the entrance to the highway.

"The parkway is the last place we want to be right now. Your new friends will have eyes everywhere within the hour looking for you, if they're not looking already," CB responded, checking his watch.

CB was proficient in a technique developed by ancient Chinese masters that he and Christian called the pin trick. By placing a pin in exactly the right place and interrupting a specific flow of energy, he could render anyone unconscious for as long as the pin remained in place. Once removed, the vital energy flow is restored, slowly taking upwards of 45 minutes for a full recovery.

CB knew well the agents and security officers would be coming out of their pin induced slumber shortly and wanted to be long gone by the time they were fully awake and realized what had happened.

He continued to drive for another ten minutes before pulling up to a small farmhouse on the far side of town.

A row of tall hedges ran along the property line masking the fields behind. Christian looked curiously at the small, dark farmhouse as they rolled to a stop.

"Why are we stopping here?" Christian asked.

"I know you well enough to know that the first thing you would want to do is see your family and Amy, so I took the liberty of renting a faster mode of transportation for us... not that that really matters. You do realize that Kearns is going to have people all over the hospital and your parents' house as soon as she finds out your missing?"

"Yeah, I know..." Christian paused, thinking about all possible scenarios, "I guess I'll have to deal with that when the time comes."

CB hopped out of the truck, grabbed a bag from behind the seat and headed toward a large barn with Christian in tow. Reaching the back of the farmhouse Christian realized what CB was talking about. The silhouette of a windsock dangling motionless against the dawn sky and an old twin engine piper sitting behind the barn, the sight of which put a smile on his face.

"I'm sure you remember how to operate one of these," CB smiled. Christian nodded affirmatively as the pair hurried toward the plane.

Wasting no time he quickly checked the plane, pulled the tube sock and chocks, then hopped into the pilot's seat and cranked her up.

Positioned for takeoff he hit the throttles, bringing the twin continentals to a deafening roar and shattering the peaceful dawn as they pulled the Seneca down the grassy field.

"Don't forget there are trees at the end of the runway... OK," CB spewed nervously. The Seneca bounced down the bumpy grass runway reaching his takeoff speed quickly. With a rebellious smirk, Christian listened carefully to his co-pilot's continued whining.

"You see the trees... right? Cutting it kind of close aren't you?" a jittery CB yelped as they drew closer to the end of the rural runway.

"Maybe a little," he smiled, pulling back the yoke just shy of the tree line with his eyes still on his co-pilot.

"What the hell are you looking at?" CB bitched, his focus bouncing between Christian and the rapidly approaching wall of trees.

"Look that way!" he yelled, pointing forward. "Oh-oh-oh..." Seeing nothing but trees in front of him, CB grabbed the dash and closed his eyes.

Christian pulled up, laughing at the cries of his co-pilot, payback for his little game back in the holding cell.

"You crazy son of a bitch! What the hell is wrong with you?" CB cringed as the treetops scraped the bottom of the plane. "P-h-e-w -- I swear we were going to hit that time," he said, wiping the cold sweat from his brow. "Jesus, I think I have to change my shorts... And how do you expect me to explain why we have branches hanging off the landing gear?"

CB could fly, but he felt it somehow unnatural, a fact that Christian knew all too well. He sported a mischievous smirk on his face and was grateful for the rare opportunity to scare the hell out of him.

Christian focused on the flight, keeping the Seneca well below five hundred feet as they headed east out and over the Atlantic. A few miles offshore he climbed to altitude and took a northeast heading toward HTO.

Tensions were high as they discussed their plans to visit the hospital. Christian's underlying guilt for what had happened to Amy trumped any concerns about Kearns and the goons she was sure to deploy once she found him missing. It was now a race against time.

Christian's approach to Hampton Airport afforded the opportunity to carefully examine the area surrounding the airport and the hospital, looking for any unusual activity. The one thing similar about law enforcement and agency vehicles is that they both stand out from the air, especially in less densely populated areas. Large numbers on the roof of law enforcement vehicles were easy to spot and the agency cars rarely traveled alone and would look like a stream of carpenter ants heading to and from their prey, making them easily visible passing through the rural grasslands surrounding the airport.

Landing the Seneca he taxied to the FBO, the airport service area, and shut down the continentals. As he climbed out of the plane he was startled by three familiar voices calling to him. Looking up with surprise he saw Tweet, Connor and Maddy running toward him.

"What's going on?" he asked CB telepathically.

"We needed a ride, so I made a call," CB smiled.

"But I thought you said I shouldn't..."

CB interrupted, "I know we shouldn't let anyone know about us, especially friends and family, but I didn't tell them anything about us. All they know is what they think they saw on New Year's Eve, and that we would be arriving this morning to visit Amy, nothing else. And besides, after I saw what they saw through your eyes and what they did for you, I thought it was safe enough to ask for a ride."

CB stepped back just as Tweet and Conner jumped Christian, welcoming him home. The boys dominating the meet up, Maddy waited patiently for her chance to greet him properly. Her eyes welled up as she lost her battle to hold back the tears. Christian glanced at her fondly. Her cheeks wet with tears, he reached out and pulled her in for a hug.

"It's so good to see you," she whispered to him, squeezing him tight and pressing her cold, wet cheek to his.

"It's great to see you too," Christian said softly, a look of concern on his face. "What are you guys doing here? You can get into serious trouble if anyone finds out you even saw me."

"Don't worry about us, we can take care of ourselves," Connor jumped in, boasting proudly and with a little dramatic license, reminding them all just one more time that he was Tazed... and survived.

Following the quick reunion they went their separate ways. Tweet, Connor and Maddy left in Tweet's car, and Christian and CB headed out of the airport in Connor's newly restored nineteen-seventy Monte Carlo.

"I hope they don't scratch it," he whimpered, watching nervously as his car turned out of the airport and disappeared. After years of effort, his Christmas present was the new paint job that adorned the almost perfect restoration.

"I wouldn't worry about it, they're only going to the hospital and coming back here. What could go wrong in a half hour?" Tweet assured him with Maddy nodding affirmatively in support.

– Two –
And Then There Were Two

A serious yet confident Pamela Kearns arrived earlier than usual at the unassuming building housing the ultra-secretive government agency. It drew little attention as it looked like every other building surrounding the airport, but this one was home for a group that conducted unorthodox operations outside of executive knowledge around the world, searching for anything or anyone that would provide an edge for our government, especially those with unique talents.

She was optimistic that today would be the day that Christian broke his silence. The guard's recent reports indicated Christian had been speaking to himself, day and night. This was good news to her. Psychologically she assumed this meant Christian was showing signs of breaking down, longing for interaction with other people after his sixty day confinement in solitary. The fact that the guards heard him speaking to himself through the night also made her believe that he was suffering with time disorientation, a sign of extreme stress and anxiety, among other things. What she was unaware of was that he was training night and day by searching the recesses of his mind to increase his skills and knowledge from his many past lives. Not having the benefit of the surveillance equipment Christian disabled telepathically while training, the fleeting moments the guards listened in on him were providing a less than accurate description of her prisoner's state of mind.

Her past experience in dealing with similarly gifted and unwilling individuals had taught her that locking him away in solitary with no contact with the outside world would eventually break him. She thought she was getting close to opening communications with him. It would be the first time anyone talked to him since she confined him for refusing to answer her questions. Her anticipation that today would be the day fueled her expectations.

She played out the scenario over and over in her mind as she pulled into the facility and flashed her ID without noticing the unresponsive guard.

"How am I going to approach him? What should I say? This is going to be his first contact with anyone in close to sixty days. OK, I'll ask him how he is and what he's feeling before I ask him if he's ready to talk. No-No-No that's too easy... I'll ask him if he's ready to talk first. Then if I don't like his response, I'll just walk away... Yeah! That's it, I'll ask him through the door. I won't even open it. He'll feel helpless..." she paused. "He must want to get out – fifty-seven days in solitary would drive anyone to the edge. I'll tell him the only way he's going to see daylight is by talking to me. But what if he says no? No matter, he's not going anywhere anyway," she smiled confidently, pulling into her parking spot. "I'll break him if it's the last thing I do."

"I can't wait to hear the guards' report on what he was up to last night." With growing anticipation she hurried through the lot to the front of the building and entered.

Her eyes focused on the empty chair at the guard station, "What the hell... where are the guards?" she thought, her confidence fading as curiosity and concern kicked in.

"What's going on?" she questioned herself, looking up and down the eerily quiet hallways.

"Where the hell is everyone?" she yelled. They were missing. In fact, everyone was missing. A shiver coursed through her as her voice echoed in the narrow corridors. A rush of panic overcame her as she ran to the back office. No one was there either.

Then the unimaginable crossed her mind, "No, it can't be." She ran toward the elevator and pushed the button repeatedly. "Damn it!" she growled, noticing the elevator was coming up from the third level below, the holding cells. She greeted an unsuspecting guard with a cold hard glare as the doors opened.

"What the hell is going on? Where is everyone?" she barked.

His jaw dropped when he saw her face and her eyes locked on him like a predator that had cornered its prey. Standing in stunned silence with a paled face he summoned the courage to tell her.

"Well – where is everyone?" she blasted him again.

"He... He's gone," the guard stuttered.

"Who's gone?" Kearns demanded, praying he wasn't referring to Christian.

"The boy... he's gone."

Kearns' face flushed, the veins in her neck and across her forehead swelled under her pressure-driven anger. She pushed him backward into the elevator with a snarl and slammed the button for lower level three. With fire in her eyes she grilled him for information on the way down to the holding cells. It was the longest ride of his life.

The tension escalated as the doors opened and Pamela stepped out onto the floor to see security combing every inch of the small detaining area. Her mere presence stopped the flurry of activity.

"Everyone, here now," she bellowed.

"Not you," she scowled at the nervous guard who had just gathered the courage to step through the elevator doorway behind her. She shoved him back into the elevator, "You get your incompetent ass upstairs and watch the front. No one comes in or goes out... got it? This is supposed to be one of the most secure facilities on the god damned planet, let's pretend like it is," she barked and turned slowly to face the remaining guards as the elevator doors closed behind her, determined to get to the bottom of what happened.

The guards hastily gathered themselves in front of the outer doors to the holding cells.

"Who's going to tell me what the hell happened?" she snapped angrily with growing impatience. The first of the reluctant guards stepped forward.

"We don't know ma'am," he said with dread in his eyes.

"What did you say?"

"We don't know ma'am," the guard replied.

"You mean to tell me, not one of you, the most highly trained security and field agents in the country, can tell me how a college kid unlocked a three hundred pound steel door with a coded key lock and got past six of you and strolled out the front door without so much as a 'how do you do'? Really? Not one of you?" she asked with disgust.

Another guard stepped forward.

"What do you want?" Kearns asked pacing.

"I thought you should know that I reviewed the tapes," he said.

"Oh, you reviewed the tapes did you?" Kearns mocked, "and let me guess – you found nothing but static and fuzz from the moment the cell door opened?"

"Well, yes ma'am," the guard replied as a disgusted Kearns turned to walk away.

"But there's one more thing... the tapes stopped working an hour and a half before we woke up."

Pamela stopped in her tracks, "Before you woke up?" she asked with angry curiosity.

"Yes ma'am, we all woke up about the same time," the guard replied.

"So all of you were asleep at the same time?" she inquired.

"Yes ma'am. They must have used nerve gas on us or something," the guard added.

"Nerve gas," Kearns mocked. "And what time did you wake up?"

"About an hour ago," the guard quivered. "But none of us could move until a few minutes ago."

"An hour ago? An hour ago?" she repeated angrily. "Did any of you idiots even think of picking up a god damned phone?" Kearns blew up. "Bring the discs to my office, NOW," she demanded as she boarded the elevator.

Within minutes of Kearns reaching her office, the security discs were delivered. As she reviewed the video at speed she came across something interesting. A momentary break in the distortion on the footage revealed the legs of a person entering the elevator just after four in the morning. She could see that the unknown intruder boarding the elevator was not wearing standard agency attire, nor was he wearing prison scrubs; he was wearing blue jeans and light purple sneakers. The rest was a blur. She paused the video and studied it for a moment.

It was enough to estimate the size of the intruder's foot and his approximate height, but it told her something much more interesting... it told her Christian had help from the outside.

The guard interjected, "I found something else that may interest you when I reviewed the footage," he said rewinding the video. He showed Kearns the footage from outside the perimeter of the facility just before the cameras went blank about 4 a.m. "Look at this, in the top left corner. It's a car."

"So, it's a car. So what, there's lots of cars in and out of here all the time. We're near the airport, or did you forget that?" Kearns replied sarcastically.

The optimistic guard continued, "I know, but look at this... this car follows the timeline. One and a half hours later, there it is again driving away from the entrance. The cameras stopped working when this car reached this point and then, one and a half hours later the same car passes the same location and the cameras start to function again. That's more than coincidental. It could be them," he said confidently.

"Them?" Kearns looked at him inquisitively.

"Yes them – Wait..." The guard continued. "There's one more thing..." Kearns listened intently. "If the kid was in his cell and the cameras went out starting from the outside first, then that means that his accomplice is another one of them, him... them," he stumbled.

"What do you mean, one of them?" Kearns inquired, feigning ignorance.

The guard proceeded cautiously with his explanation, knowing all too well just how secretive Kearns was, especially with this particular case.

"When you brought this kid in, I was working the security monitors for the interrogation room. I saw the screens go blank when you entered the room. We spoke, do you remember?"

"Continue," Kearns stared blankly.

"Then, as soon as you left the room the cameras came back on. So whatever it is that he did or does to the cameras, just like he's been doing to our surveillance equipment on the third floor since he got here, this guy can do too. They're the same."

"It could be..." she murmured to herself, perking up a bit.

AND THEN THERE WERE TWO

"Can you enhance this from this distance?" she asked, backing the video up to a rear view of the car.

"Not here ma'am, but I'll bring it to the lab and work on it," he replied.

"I want to know everything about that car in twenty minutes," she ordered, "and give me a close up of the elevator shot too."

"Yes ma'am."

"And sergeant."

"Ma'am?"

"...tell no one, got it?"

"Yes ma'am!" he replied and hurried off to the lab.

"And then there were two," she murmured with a renewed sense of hope and a knowing grin. If she were able to capture two of them, she could learn how they interact, study them, dissect them if necessary to learn of their abilities. Her moment was interrupted by a knock on the door. Another security officer entered.

"Ma'am, we thought you should see this," he said.

"What is it?" she asked.

"Not sure, ma'am. All we know is it doesn't come from anything around here. We found it under one of the guard desks," he said, handing her a small needle with colorful thread wrapped around one end of it.

"Which desk?" she asked.

"The front desk ma'am," he replied as Pamela inspected the find.

"Take this to the lab and tell them I want to know everything about it A-S-A-P."

"Yes ma'am," he said and rushed out the door.

Taking a deep breath she picked up the phone, "Get me Colonel Barton."

"Yes ma'am," the operator responded as Kearns waited impatiently.

"Ma'am, the colonel is in an early conference with 'Sec Def'."

"I don't care if he's taking a bath with the president... I need you to get him on the phone now," she demanded.

An agitated Barton picked up the phone, "This better be good," he said sternly in a raspy voice.

Kearns explained the situation to him. Barton was furious at the loss of such a prize, his loud response disturbing the ongoing conference with the Sec Def more than once; however, he calmed down a bit after learning of the prospect of capturing two of the elusive members of the fraternity.

"I don't care what you have to do to... I want them both collected within 24 hours! Got it?" he yelled, disturbing the Sec Def one last time. "I want hourly updates," he demanded and returned to the conference.

Time passed quickly as she planned her next move, more determined than ever to capture Christian, and now his accomplice. She ordered Davenport and the New York agents to cover Christian's home and the hospital where Amy lay in her medically induced coma. Before she knew it, there was another knock on the door. The officer walked in confident she would be happy with the reports.

She opened the envelope and read the first part of the report regarding the needle. It was an unmarked needle commonly used in acupuncture and other Eastern healing techniques, and available from a multitude of suppliers and distributors making it difficult to trace, however, there was one very unique detail about the needle.

The silk thread wrapped around it originated in Thailand, but not from the silkworms of Khorat in northeastern Thailand, the center of the silk industry. This silk was made from a wasp's nest known only in southern Thailand. The traces of blood belonged to Donald Kefir, head of security.

"Hmmm, another piece of the puzzle," she thought. "Find out any and all distribution avenues that would carry this specific type of needle with this specific type of silk threading," Kearns said, realizing that such rare silk would most likely be uncommon, and only available in high end or specialty shops.

She opened the second folder, and a smile crossed her face. "Gotcha both," she gloated as she reviewed the contents. She had everything she wanted, a clear close up of the elevator shot and the description of the car, the license plate and registration information. She wasted no time picking up the phone and ordering Channing's team to the address for surveillance and placing an APB out on the car with orders for local law enforcement to locate and inform only.

– Three –
The Redemption

Christian and CB arrived at the hospital and cautiously circled the perimeter to see if there was any unusual activity in the area. Not sensing immediate danger, the pair parked their new ride on the far side of the lot and made their way to the back of the hospital, entering through an employee's utility entrance to avoid being seen.

Christian was battling his emotions as they cautiously made their way to his father's office, a battle that only intensified as they waited for Dr. Asher to return to his office.

Although excited at the prospect of seeing his father, he was tormented with what had happened and with his increasing desire for revenge. His only saving grace was a secretive personal moment shared with Hwei Ru. She was the oldest in the group of similarly gifted individuals who possessed amazing abilities that only age can bring. When CB was teaching Christian to connect to others telepathically, Hwei Ru was his first connection. She shared a vision with him, a glimpse of things to come that she requested he not share with anyone, including CB.

The reunion with his father was short and bittersweet. Christian was shattered by the news his father shared regarding the Kendall's decision to give Amy up to God. They would be arriving soon to say their final goodbyes. Edward could see how tortured he was hearing the news and arranged for him to see his mother shortly before John and Debra Kendall arrived, with the hope that her presence would somehow be of comfort to him.

Katheryn, surprised to see him, greeted him with tears. Their time together was brief, cut short by the early arrival of the Kendalls who were anxious to release Amy from her suffering.

Christian was at her side, caressing her hand as the doctors began to remove Amy's life support. Katheryn watched her son with growing concern. She knew how painful this was for him, but he wasn't showing it. His hard, cold appearance frightened her as she had never before seen her son emotionless. She knew well that he felt responsible for her death and feared what may happen.

One tear rolled down his cheek as the heart monitor flat-lined with its distinctive long beep. It was over. Keeping his composure amidst the emotional breakdown of the small group, he said his final goodbyes to Amy and fell silent. His persistent stoic appearance alarmed Katheryn as he hugged her coldly, bid them all farewell, and walked away quickly with a flood of emotions surging through him fueling his desire for revenge.

Katheryn wept as Christian disappeared through the stairwell entrance. Resting her head on Edward's shoulder she spoke her heart whispering, "I lost two children today."

CB tried to comfort his unresponsive friend as they made their way down the stairwell to the exit at the back of the hospital. He too had growing concern as he glanced at Christian. He had seen that look before... many times in men fighting the same relentless battle, plagued by the torment of the inner conflict playing out within his mind, a battle between what was right and his desire for revenge. His face told it all.

"Phew," a muffled sigh of relief crossed CB's lips as they exited the building and made their way to the car, his fears abated for the moment. But not for long.

Christian grabbed his arm and pulled him to a stop.

"Son of a bitch... we were almost out of here," CB murmured to himself, looking at Christian knowing that his thirst for revenge had won the battle. The battle was over, a sheer unyielding look of determination filled Christian's face and the decision that CB feared would seal his fate had been made.

CB immediately tried to open a telepathic connection to Christian, but was blocked. Whatever it was Christian was planning he wasn't willing to share.

"Wait! There's something else I have to do!" he said with conviction.

Christian continued to block CB from connecting. CB, whose fear of what may happen next swelled, had to ask even though he was afraid of what Christian's response would be, "What's on your mind?" There was no response.

CB followed as Christian turned back to the hospital. His inner alarm was sounding as he continued to study the hard, focused look on his friend's face, attempting to somehow decipher what exactly was going to happen next.

His stomach churning and ready to heave at the decision he had just made, Christian gave his reply, "There's one more person I need to visit to before I leave." He swallowed hard to suppress the mass of acidic chyme creeping its way up his throat.

"NOW? Are you sure you want to do this... NOW? The agency is going to be crawling all over this place before you know it," CB protested, attempting to dissuade him from what he thought was sure to happen.

Christian nodded affirmatively, "Yes, now. We'll be fine. Why don't you wait down here?" he suggested, blowing off CB's concerns.

"No, no... that's OK – I'll go with you," CB blurted nervously, his tone turning softer as his head dropped in dejection. "We've always had each other's back no matter what, right? No reason to stop now."

Christian, as if by instinct, led CB up the back stairwell to the fifth floor. Entering the hallway he turned and proceeded through the tarps covering the entrance into the east wing of the hospital that was under renovation. The rooms in this wing were unoccupied for the renovation except for one, which was being used for Morano, the trigger man who shot the dart that pierced Amy's skull.

In a coma since Christian unleashed his wrath that fateful New Year's Eve, Morano had been sequestered on the fifth floor at the agency's request. It was almost perfect.

They moved cautiously down the eerily quiet hallway, the occasional crackling of the odd piece of construction debris beneath their feet echoed loudly in the narrow corridor.

"Wait here," he said, slipping through a door and leaving his apprehensive friend behind. The unmistakable click of the door locking echoed in the hallway.

CB paced anxiously. For the first time in as far back as he could remember he had no idea what Christian was going to do. Only guesses, especially in the state of mind he was in after seeing Amy pass. All he knew was that whatever was going to happen behind that closed door, good or bad, would decide Christian's fate, and it was his decision alone to make.

He sighed with helplessness as he reflected on the exchange of words Christian had with Van Dunne on the very topic of his fate. Van Dunne is an enigma; powerful beyond aristocracy, monarchs and presidents. He controls most everything that happens on the planet between world leaders, both financially and politically, as well as other worldly interests. Christian's unusual circumstance, being awakened so late in life, drew the attention of Van Dunne who extended an undesirable invitation to assess this unusual young man. During their unprecedented meeting he shared with Christian the technology with which he monitored the other members of this fraternity and the fate that would befall any member who used their gifts for purposes outside of those that were for the good of the planet and its inhabitants. He has the power of life or death over all members of this extraordinary group, including Christian.

CB's thoughts then turned to the many lifetimes they had shared, fearing that this one may soon be near its end. He paced aimlessly, worrying, afraid for what may happen to his friend.

He dragged himself down the hall to a sitting room with a window facing the front of the hospital and flopped into a dust covered chair to continue with his thoughts. His moment was soon interrupted. Startled by a horrific sound, he sprang up from his seat. The eerie, shrill sound emanating from the room echoed through the hallway, sending shivers through his spine and alerting the nursing staff down the corridor in the west wing. Fearing the worst was happening, he dropped his head in dismay asking himself, "Why?"

The eerie shrill sound now silenced, he lifted his head and looked through the window to see a line of agency cars filing into the parking lot and splitting off to cover every section of the grounds. He watched as a dozen agency cars lined up in front of the hospital with a pair of agency men in each. Out in front of them all was Davenport, one of the local agency men. He aggressively barked orders to the occupants of each car.

Time was short for the pair. The agents would be on the fifth floor before they knew it. CB hurried back to the room, reaching it just as Christian opened the door with tear-filled eyes and a look of exhaustion. CB's fears were confirmed as he gazed upon the limp, motionless half-covered body lying on the hospital bed. The smell of ozone filled the room. CB's disappointment was apparent; this wasn't at all like his friend.

"C'mon, there's no time to lose. Follow me..." CB barked as the elevator bell sounded, alerting him the agents had reached the fifth floor already. He could hear them talking to the nursing staff as they made their way toward the tarped-off hallway. Their silhouettes appeared, darkening the opaque tarp as they reached to separate the barrier between them and the hallway leading to their fallen friend's room.

"Get in here, hurry," he said, pulling Christian into a vacant room.

Listening intently, his ear pressed against the inside of the door, he waited for the agents to enter Morano's room. Once inside he pulled his weary friend out of the room and down the hall, ducking in and out of rooms and alcoves as they cautiously made their way to the utility stairwell at the back of the hospital.

"What the hell is wrong with you?" he growled, struggling to pull his lethargic friend down the hallway. There was no reply. It struck him momentarily that he had seen this type of behavior before when another had used skills which were far more advanced than Christian should have, but only once, and that was lifetimes ago with one of the original seven. "This is impossible... It can't be," he thought. "Christian is nowhere near advanced enough for that, so what the hell is happening here?" His curiosity faded as he focused more on surviving the moment.

He pulled Christian into the stairwell. His concentration was increasing but his energy was slow to return as they stumbled their way down to the fourth floor landing. They could hear a sudden flurry of activity from agents in the corridors above and below them echoing through the stairwell.

Christian pointed to a narrow utility room door, "Go in here."

CB pulled the door open, "In here... Are you crazy?" he asked, almost protesting the suggestion. "You know this will be the first place they look. Where the hell can we go from here?"

Christian shushed him and they entered the small utility room. He opened the ventilation service door accessing the large vertical shaft of the heating system and listened quietly to everything going on above and below them.

"I used to hide from my father in here as a kid," Christian smiled, reflecting. Only a moment had passed before they heard one of the agents say, "What? He was where? How long ago? Listen up everyone, Zeus is onsite. I repeat, Zeus is on site. Lock it down, no one goes in or out. Got it?" the agent commanded.

"Now what?" CB asked, listening as the noise from the agents actively searching room to room got closer to the stairwell.

"Take off your coat."

"My coat?" CB asked with a puzzled look on his face.

"Just take it off... Now lay it down right here." Christian pointed to the horizontal ventilation shaft that ran the full length of the building, smiling deviously. "Now help me with this," he said pointing to a welder's tank in the corner. CB strained to pick up the tank with little help from his recovering friend. "Now slide it in base first on top of the coat," Christian directed.

CB smiled as he slid the tank onto his jacket lying on the edge of the horizontal vent. Christian handed him a medium sized pipe wrench and started to climb into the vertical vent shaft.

"What are you doing?" CB asked. "You're going to kill yourself. "

"Take the pipe wrench and climb in behind me and don't worry, I used to slide down these shafts all the time when I was younger," Christian said, sliding halfway down the shaft between floors, straining with feet and arms pressed against the inside of the vent wall to support his weight.

"You're not thinking what I think you're thinking... are you? " CB asked apprehensively. Christian smiled. "You are one crazy SOB," CB blurted, climbing into the shaft and pulling the vent door closed.

"You do know this is an oxy-acetylene tank, don't you... One spark and Ka-Boom?" CB asked, his voice echoing.

"Yep, you'd better hit it clean as you're dropping," Christian grunted, straining to hold his position in the shaft.

"Dropping? Very funny. What are we really going to do?"

Christian replied with silence.

"I can't believe you're serious! We're on the fourth floor," CB said, hurrying to wrap the wrench in a rag to prevent sparks from the strike from igniting the contents of the tank. "Crazy bastard... you're going to get us both killed!" he griped.

"Trust me, we'll be fine. I've done this hundreds of times," Christian exaggerated. "Let me know when you're ready; we'll do it on three, OK?" Christian's voice echoed in the shaft.

"Ready!" CB responded, shaking his head at this crazy idea and beginning his countdown.

"O-N-E... THREE," CB's countdown was cut short when heard the third floor stairwell door burst open. Letting go of his grip, he dropped down on top of Christian's head and with one hard swing snapped the valve clean off the top of the tank. The high pressure tank screamed as it released a plume of noxious gas through the jagged opening and started to rocket along the horizontal shaft.

Christian, losing his hold, dropped and the pair plummeted down the ventilation shaft. His escape would not be as smooth as he remembered from childhood. With building velocity, panic set in as he remembered the large exhaust fan that lay at the end of the shaft.

"Oh No, Oh No, Oh Nooo," he cried as they dropped. His heart pounded as they hit the curve at the bottom of the vent shaft at velocity.

As a child, the curve slowed him to a stop, but he'd have no such luck today. His eyes widened as he slid through the curve and focused on the flashing light at the end of the vent. Mustering every ounce of strength he had, he strained to slow their momentum before his feet hit the stabilizing bars used to prevent the vent from collapsing under the weight of the enormous unprotected fan blades spinning hard to pump hot air through the system.

"You OK? Phew," Christian sighed, relieved as he leaned to his side, searching for the latch to the service door that would free them from the blast of hot air pushing through the blades.

"One... three, what the hell happened to two?" Christian asked sarcastically.

"Are you kidding? This was your plan! Launch an explosive tank through the vent and then drop four floors through a greasy old shaft. Are you out of your freaking mind?" CB ranted in a suppressed tone.

"Relax, I used to play in here all the time, but this was the first time I dropped four floors," Christian chuckled, relieved.

"What the hell does that mean?" CB asked.

"Oh – I only made it to the second floor before my father caught me and made me promise never to do it again and then grounded me for life," he snickered. "That's how I knew there was a curve at the bottom to slow us down. I forgot about the fan though," he reflected. "It worked a lot better when I was eight."

"You could have mentioned that," CB suggested.

Hearing the commotion in the walls the agents raced up the stairwell with guns drawn, making the fourth floor landing in seconds. They threw open the utility closet door finding nothing was askew, but the loud banging sound in the vents peaked their interest and gave cause to alert the other agents. "They're in the ventilation system... fourth floor."

Cautiously they pulled open the vent service door. The deafening hiss of the pressurized acetylene escaping the tank and the thunderous sound of the tank slamming off the vent walls echoed within, covering Christian and CB's descent.

Agents raced down the hallways chasing the rumbling sound to the far end of the building. Reaching the end of the line, the tank burst through the outside service door and jetted into the small power plant adjacent to the hospital. The violent explosion sent startled agents, patients and staff fleeing for the lives. The forceful blast shattered windows, set off car alarms, and sent shrapnel screaming through the air that severed two powerlines, causing them to pop loudly as they danced across the pavement.

"What the hell was that?" Davenport clicked in demanding to know and looking toward the explosion. Agents on the fifth floor chimed in with the explanation.

"Nice distraction," Davenport thought, scanning the perimeter for any sign of Christian.

Dr. Asher glanced at the nervous orderly. "What's so important that you had to drag me away from my wife and the Kendalls?

"She's alive," the pale orderly pointed at the gurney. "She's alive, I saw her move."

"I would think by now you know that bodies can twitch for some time after passing." Dr. Asher answered with an annoyed tone.

"No... it wasn't a twitch, she moved," the orderly argued. "Look, there it is again."

Glancing at the gurney he saw movement under the sheet. "This is impossible. There must be some logical explanation." Edward stuttered grabbing the sheet and pulling it down slowly.

The orderly stood in the background blessing himself repeatedly. "Oh Dios mio."

"Hurry," Dr. Asher ordered, "get her into operatory three... stat."

Dr. Asher hastily checked vitals as they maneuvered the gurney across the hallway and into operatory three. Drawing the curtains closed for privacy, he continued to monitor Amy's vitals which were growing stronger at a remarkable rate. Everything he knew from his training and clinical experience told him this was impossible, but it was happening in front of his eyes.

The orderly pushed a crash cart through the curtains, just in case. Realizing Dr. Asher hadn't summoned a nurse yet he asked, "Did you want me to get the nurses to help you?"

"No, I don't want anyone to know what's happening," Edward replied, staying focused on Amy. "Do you know what an EKG and EEG are?" he asked.

"Yes sir," the orderly replied. "Electrocardiogram and electroencephalogram."

"Find them and bring them to me quietly. I don't want to alert anyone to what's happening here," Dr. Asher requested.

Upon his return, Dr. Asher looked at the orderly, "I want you to swear that you will tell no one of this. Got it? NO ONE!"

"I swear, I won't tell a soul," the orderly said as he blessed himself.

"Go get the Kendalls and my wife; they're in the front waiting room... and don't let anyone see you looking so nervous."

"Yes sir," the orderly responded, and hurried out of the operatory.

Edward began to question everything he had learned in all his years of practice. Even remembering the many discussions he had with his old friend Dr. Stedwell concerning the fraternity and their special gifts, he could never have imagined what he had just witnessed was possible. "But how? Did it have to do with the mysterious visitors today?" he wondered. All he knew was that what he had seen defied medical science. It was, in a word, a miracle.

The orderly escorted the Kendalls and Katheryn to the operatory, making sure not to draw the attention of the agents actively searching the hospital. More concerned with the flurry of activity, he ignored the exasperated Mr. Kendall's questions. Upset already and having no idea why they were summoned, he was less than pleasant with his demands.

Mrs. Kendall moved slowly, the grief of her loss was evidenced by the ongoing stream of tears and her lethargic gait as she leaned on her husband for support. Just as they reached the operatory the lights flickered off and on for the last time before all went dark, a result of the damaged power lines.

"What the hell is going on here?" a startled John Kendall asked Katheryn.

"I don't know," she replied as a cold shiver coursed through her. Her focus turned to thoughts of Christian, knowing something wasn't right. Her motherly instincts kicked in as they had many times in the past when Christian got deep into something he shouldn't have.

The emergency lighting strained to come on, allowing the grieving parents and Katheryn to continue on into the operatory. Katheryn's concern intensified as she watched the lights slowly power to full brightness, the effects of an underpowered generator pushing power through an antiquated backup system trying to power an overloaded system.

"What's going on?" she asked Edward as the lights flickered under the power of the emergency generators. Edward answered with subdued elation, "You're not going to believe this... wait here a moment." He excused himself and walked behind the curtain to check on Amy.

Amy, weak from her miraculous re-animation asked, "Where's Christian? I can feel him... he's close by." She paused, fading in and out momentarily. "I felt his kiss," she smiled feebly.

Dr. Asher shushed her, "Save your strength honey, he's fine," he shared unknowingly. "I have someone else who wants to see you." He stepped out from behind the curtain and motioned for the Kendalls and Katheryn to join him.

Mr. and Mrs. Kendall approached Edward, unsure of why they had been summoned. "What's this all about?" Mr. Kendall asked in a semi-harsh tone staring directly at Edward, "My wife can't handle much more of this."

Edward smiled and stepped back away from the gurney. Amy's soft glance filled him with a faith and elation that was previously unknown to him. "Oh my god!!! What... How is this possible?" he burst, grabbing Amy's hand. His stoic face softened instantly and his eyes welled. "Oh God... Thank you, thank you, thank you!" he praised.

Mrs. Kendall's soul filled with joy seeing Amy's sparkling eyes open and filled with life. She didn't understand how or why... she didn't care, her prayers had been answered. She showered Amy with kisses and gave thanks for this miracle.

Katheryn cradled up to Edward with a wide smile and tears of joy running down her cheeks, amazed at the miracle she was witnessing. She looked to Edward for answers he did not have and then blessed herself.

Edward stared in wonderment as Amy's strength returned at an inexplicable rate, challenging all he had ever learned.

"Dr. Asher, Dr. Asher," the orderly hurried in, "Some guys in suits are looking for you. They want..." the orderly stopped and pulled Edward to the side whispering, "They want to see the girl's body. What are you going to do?"

"Don't worry about that. Distract them for me and don't tell them anything that you've seen. As far as you know, none of this happened. Got It?"

"Yes sir!"

"Go back to the lobby and have me paged from the nurse's station. I'll be out in a minute."

"OK," he responded and hurried back to the lobby.

After some effort Edward was able to get the attention of the Kendall's and in a serious tone said, "I'm going to ask you both to do something you won't understand and I need you to trust me."

"What are we talking about?" John Kendall asked.

"This is a military hospital and there are agents looking for someone. I need you to follow Katheryn back to the lobby. It's very important that you appear sad to them and above all, let no one know what has happened here."

Appalled by the mere suggestion they protested his request, but Edward persisted. When Mrs. Kendall saw the serious and overly concerned look on his face, she reluctantly agreed.

"What's this got to do with my daughter?" Mr. Kendall asked demandingly.

Edward paused.

"I can't explain everything to you now, but I think we all consider this a miracle... and if they catch wind of this, they'll want to know more and I don't wish that for you or for Amy.

"They wouldn't dare touch her," Mrs. Kendall said with a determined look on her face.

Edward continued, "They're the government. They will do whatever they want until they know everything and more about the situation. You're ex-military, John. You know what these types are capable of."

John Kendall realized the seriousness of the situation and accepted the explanation, urging his wife to as well. Debra was not as understanding of the explanation and could care less about the government and what they wanted. Even after having agreed with the request she found herself unwilling to leave her daughter's side until she felt a delicate grip squeeze her arm. She looked at Amy with both joy and sadness.

"Mom, do what they ask. It's important to me... don't worry, I'll be fine," Amy smiled gently.

"OK honey," Mrs. Kendall agreed, wiping her tears. She kissed Amy one more time before taking John's arm to leave the operatory.

As the Kendalls stepped out from behind the curtain Edward turned to Amy, "Sweetheart, there are some government people here looking for Christian. Do you understand?" he asked.

"I know," Amy replied weakly.

"OK honey... this is what I want you to do."

"I know this is going to sound strange but I'm going to cover you for a few minutes and all you have to do is not move." Edward continued to explain to Amy what she needed to do and not to be afraid. He covered her with the sheet and whispered, "You'll be fine honey," just as the nurse's page for him came over the intercom. He stepped out from behind the curtain to find a surprise waiting for him. The agents had already arrived and had stopped Katheryn and the Kendalls by the door.

Three suits approached him with the usual disregard for anyone other than themselves. "Dr. Asher?" The agent questioned, receiving an affirmative nod from Edward.

"How can I help you?" he inquired.

"I am agent Tully. We need to speak with you."

"I'll be with you in a minute," Edward replied.

"We need to speak with you N-O-W," the agent said with a demanding tone.

Edward excused himself and motioned for Katheryn to take the Kendalls to the sitting room. He knew she would ensure that they continued to appear as if they were grieving.

"Who were you talking to back there?" Agent Tully asked. Edward fought his urge to verbally strike out at the agents. Calm and collected he replied, "I was just saying my final goodbyes to my son's girlfriend. You remember her; one of you put a dart in her head."

"An unfortunate turn of events," Tully replied coldly, disregarding the comment without the least bit of sympathy.

"I will need to see her body."

"Haven't you guys done enough to this family already? What more do you want?" Edward protested, glaring at Tully.

"Step aside Doctor," Tully physically moved Edward to the side and opened the curtain.

"Is this her?" he asked, reaching for the sheet covering her body.

"Yes," Edward replied, grabbing Tully's arm and restating, "Haven't you done enough to hurt this family? Let her rest in peace for god's sake."

Tully gave Edward yet another cold, emotionless stare as he yanked his arm free and pulled back the sheet to view Amy's body.

Edward was shocked with what he saw when Tully pulled the sheet back. Amy's face and neck were cyanotic, a telltale sign of oxygen deprivation that resulted in a blue-gray coloring.

He panicked inside, knowing time was of the essence. If she was to be resuscitated, he had to get rid of Tully and his goons first.

"This her?" Tully asked another agent who was present the night of the "incident."

"Yes sir, that's her." He looked away, remorseful for his small part in the event.

"What a shame... waste of a nice piece of ass, don't you think?" he smugly stated with an uncaring grin, snapping a pic and throwing the sheet back over her head.

Edward strained to keep his composure. His blood boiled at the lewd comment and he stepped toward Tully aggressively, ready to strike, only to pull himself back at the last second. He needed them out of there.

"What... you got something to say Doc?" Tully glowered at Edward who kept his composure and requested the agent leave her to rest in peace, then escorted them to the door. As soon as they exited he rushed to Amy's side. His only thoughts were, "How horrible it would be to put the Kendalls through this a second time." He felt sure they would both snap if they had lost their daughter twice in one day.

He pulled the curtain back and ripped the sheet off of Amy, ready to resuscitate her, but he was too late. Amy opened her eyes and smiled weakly.

"Everything OK?" she asked with a soft voice.

"Yes," a curious and relieved Dr. Asher replied, "How did you do that?"

"Do what?" Amy inquired.

"Nothing, nothing at all. Just rest quietly until I come for you. Everything is going to be fine... you've been through a lot," he smiled.

Dr. Asher called to the orderly, "No one goes into operatory three... got it? I don't want anyone disturbing Ms. Kendall's body, understand? No one."

"Yes sir," the orderly responded.

Dr. Asher exited the room and headed for the waiting room. At this point he had more questions than answers. "How was this possible, where is Christian, and why did the lights go out?" Two agents watched closely as he entered the waiting area and was greeted by Katheryn.

"What the hell is going on?" she asked anxiously, "Why did they want to see her?"

"I'm not sure, but I'll find out as much as I can in a while. In the meantime, I need you to get the Kendalls out of here. Take them home with you, anywhere but here. The longer they're around the more likely someone will slip. I'm going to make her disappear."

"How?" Katheryn asked, concerned.

"I don't know yet. I'll admit her under another name, put her in another room. I don't know yet. I'll fill you in later..."

"What if they ask to see her again?" Katheryn whispered cautiously.

"I'll tell them she was sent for cremation at her family's request. She's a smart girl, she'll go along with it until I can get her out of here."

"But do you think that will really work?" Katheryn asked.

"I don't know. They've seen her already, maybe that's enough for them, but I'm not taking any chances. My guess is if we can hide her long enough, I can get her away from here. I'll figure it out. You better get going." He hurried off.

Katheryn turned to the Kendalls and requested they do what she asked without asking any questions. "I'll explain everything to you on the way home. I promise, everything is going to be alright," she assured them.

Although John and Debra couldn't understand what all the commotion was about and what it had to do with their daughter, they reluctantly agreed to go with Katheryn... for Amy's sake.

Christian, relieved to have survived the fall, pulled himself through the large service door next to the fan and jumped to the floor. Seconds later he winced hearing the sound of something hitting the fan blades, a sound that reminded him of the baseball cards he used to put in his bicycle spokes.

"Son of a bitch," echoed in the vent.

"Are you OK?" Christian asked.

CB pushed open the utility door on the side of the vent and stuck his head out, "Thanks... You could have told me you were ready to jump. Dammit look at these, I just got them and now they're ruined," he complained, swinging his feet out of the door.

Christian laughed at the site of CB's shredded purple Nike's.

With agency men scurrying through the hospital they had to move fast. It wouldn't be long before they searched the ventilation room. There was only one door, and that led to the corridor. CB cracked the door and saw agents actively searching the rooms at the end of the hallway.

"They're coming... What now?"

"It's got to be here somewhere," Christian mumbled as he peeked around to the wall behind the ventilation system.

"What, what has to be here?" CB asked. "Whatever it is, find it quick. They'll be here any minute."

"There it is, over there," Christian called to CB and started to move some boxes that were placed in front of an old door.

"What's this?" CB asked.

"This place was built in the late fifties. I remember my father showing me this when I was younger." He continued to move boxes from the front of the door with CB's help. "It's part of the bomb shelter system, you know, in case of nuclear war or if someone were to attack or bomb one of the aircraft factories that were operational around here at the time."

CB hustled to move the remaining boxes as Christian grabbed a tarp.

"What's that for?" he asked.

Christian replied with a sneaky grin as he forced open the rusty old door. He laid part of the tarp in front of the door and snaked the remainder under the door.

"Stack a few of the boxes on the tarp right up against the door while I finish this," he said, pulling the tarp through the bottom of the door.

"All set!"

"Great, get in here," he called CB into the damp, musty room.

"Help me pull the door shut... don't let the tarp get stuck." Together they pulled the rusty door closed. "Now pull the tarp slowly."

As they pulled the tarp, the boxes were pulled up against the outside of the closed door. "I remember this... s-n-e-a-k-y, didn't you pull this one on MacArthur?" CB reflected.

Before Christian could reply they heard activity on the other side of the door.

"Let's get out of here," Christian whispered. "Follow me."

He felt his way through the darkness to the back of the musty room and found what he was looking for, another door about thirty feet into the darkness. He turned the creaky old handle to unlatch the door.

"Shhhhh," CB softly shushed, concerned the piercingly loud squeaking noise would alert the agents searching only thirty feet away. They pushed the rusted old door open slowly trying not to make any noise and slipped through the narrow, moss covered opening into a long, dark corridor.

"Thank god for Ike," Christian smiled, leading the way.

The pair hurried through the darkened tunnel, feeling their way along one hundred yards of slimy, moss covered walls. CB, the brave warrior, flinched at the sound of rats scurrying under their feet as they made their way to the end of the tunnel.

"What the hell are you bitching at?" Christian asked.

"I can feel them," CB complained.

"What?" Christian asked.

"You know what you smart ass... rats! They've been jumping all around since we got into this hell hole."

"Oh yeah, I forgot about you and rats. At least they're not chickens," Christian chuckled, remembering how a maiden's father had once attacked CB with a live chicken.

"Very funny... move your ass, would you?" CB urged.

Reaching the end of the tunnel they joined together to force the old wrought iron gate open against the seasons of dirt and debris that had accumulated on the other side of the unmaintained doorway. Christian cringed as the steel gate squeaked and groaned, echoing loudly through the cold war escape route.

"Now, how do we get the car?" CB asked.

"We don't, you do!"

"Me, why me?" CB questioned.

"Because they're looking for me, not you... remember?" Christian replied.

CB climbed up the dirt berm and scanned the parking area. "This isn't going to be as easy as we thought it would be."

"What do you mean?" Christian asked, staying well behind the earthen bunker housing the tunnel exit.

"This tunnel brought us a couple of hundred feet to the north side of the hospital property and our car is parked on the south side of the hospital. And it gets better... It looks like your friend has arrived," CB reported, ducking quickly back into the tunnel.

"Kearns?" he asked.

"Yep, and here's the best part. She landed her helicopter pretty close to the car."

"How close?" Christian asked.

"About a hundred-fifty to two hundred feet – Oh there's more," CB said sarcastically. Christian, curious to see for himself, stretched his neck over the wall of earth to take a look. Not wanting to expose himself and finding his view partially obscured by shrubs he asked, "Now what?"

"They set up a command truck about fifty feet away from the car a-n-d... it looks like she's got some junior fly boys launching camera equipped drones from it."

"Hmmm..." Christian thought, "That means they can see everything. How do we get you to the car without them seeing where you came from?"

One of the drones approached, forcing them to duck back deeper into the tunnel as it passed overhead. "What next?" Christian thought.

CB chimed in, "Do you remember how long those things can stay up for?"

"About twenty to twenty five minutes, maybe less with cameras on them," Christian answered, poking his head part way out the door to see if the drone was still there. It was.

CB thought for a moment, "OK, all we have to do is wait for the drones to head back to switch the power cells. That should give us a minute or two for you to run to the tree line across the street while I work my way to the car. Sound like a plan?"

Christian nodded in agreement, "How do you plan to get to the car? You'll never make it to the car without being seen and the entire hospital has to be locked down by now."

CB paused, "That's a work in progress."

The minutes passed slowly before the drones above returned to the surveillance truck for new power packs. Christian squeezed through the partially opened door and glanced behind him. Seeing the coast was clear he made a dash for the tree line. CB followed, walking out from behind the mound of earth concealing the door and hurried toward the hospital. He was only steps away from the back entrance of the hospital when the drone returned and immediately picked up on him as he made his way into the hospital through the rear doors.

The hospital was as active as an angry hornets nest with agency personnel searching everywhere. Thinking quickly he grabbed a lab coat from the laundry and ducked into a patient's room to swipe a chart and made his way through the hospital toward the front entrance. "Almost there," he thought as he entered the lobby and his plan began to unravel. "Shit!" he mumbled under his breath and leaned up against the lobby wall, pretending to read the chart while studying the agents who were checking everyone entering and leaving the building. One of the agents noticed him lurking in the hallway fumbling through the patient's chart.

"Go check this guy out, he doesn't have a badge," he pointed at Channarong.

CB's heart began started to race. He suppressed his urge to heighten even with the increasing possibility that he may have to fight his way out. That was the last thing he wanted. Revealing himself in front of the half dozen agency personnel would put him on the agency hit list along with Christian. Time was running short, "What am I going to do?" he thought, searching for options. Undecided, CB prepared himself for the worst as the agents approached.

"Doctor Channarong, I was looking for you." Channarong smiled, relieved to hear the voice of salvation and turned slowly to see Dr. Asher walking up behind him.

Regaining his composure he replied, "Yes Dr. Asher, how may I help you?"

"I was wondering if I could discuss the Anderson case with you. We aren't sure why he wasn't responding to the treatments as expected..."

The agents interrupted, "Dr. Asher, do you know this man?"

Edward looked at them with disdain, "Of course I do. This is Dr. Channarong; he's the best neurologist we have."

"He doesn't look like a doctor to me. Where's your hospital ID? Dr. Channa... whatever. Where's your ID?" the suspicious agent questioned.

"It must have fell off in the lab... I change lab coats when I'm dissecting infectious tissue." The repulsed agent backed away.

"OK then, would you care to tell me what's wrong with this "patient" you're talking about?" the agent asked, making the quotation marks in the air with his fingers.

Dr. Asher jumped in, "He has ICP a-n..."

The agent interrupted abruptly, "I was asking Dr. Channa...

Channa-something, not you. Explain it to me Doc," the agent said snidely hoping to catch him at his own game. Channarong paused momentarily and quickly connected with Christian, sharing the moment in real time. Christian had medicine in his blood, literally. He had served as a physician in lifetimes past and had studied his father's books and journal from an early age. To him it was light reading.

"Hey, I'm in the hospital with your father and the agents are asking me something medical. Help me out."

"What the hell are you doing in the hospital? I thought you were going for the car. Tell me, what do they want to know?"

Tensions increased, "Doctor, we're waiting. Tell me what ICP is," he barked sternly as his associates moved closer.

Christian chimed in after hearing the agent's request, "Got it, ICP is intracranial pressure. Tell him this..."

Edward looked on, anxiously waiting for the long pause to end. "Say something," he thought nervously.

CB smiled smugly at the agent. "It's none of your damn business. It happens to be privileged information, but if you must know," CB gave him the finger quotes, "ICP is intracranial pressure which means increased pressure inside the cranium, skull or in your case, that melon on top of your shoulders."

Edward, both relieved and amused with CB's response bowed his head attempting to hide the grin on his face as CB continued rattling off the information Christian was providing him through their connection.

"The initial cause of the patient's problem was an oligoden-droglioma or an oligodendralglial tumor. This particular lesion is fairly rare and affects the oligodentrites, which are a form of glial cells. I'm sure you already know the supportive function of glial cells for neural tissue as well as the nutritional component they add, so I won't get into that," he said snidely.

CB looked at the glazed look on the agents face. "Hey Kojak, we're not done yet... you wanted to hear this," CB said, snapping his fingers. He could feel Christian laughing.

"When a space occupying lesion, mass or tumor grows in the cranial vault it increases ICP as does the resultant edema from said lesion being removed as this one was a few days ago, it causes swelling. Trust me, Kojak, I don't have time to give you a lesson in neuroanatomy, but if you'd like I'll bring you in with me the next time I crack open a skull. Maybe you could pick up some fava beans and make a meal of it..."

The agent, disgusted at the suggestion, gulped as he thought of his reply. There was none. CB glanced at Dr. Asher and gave him a wink.

"Will that be all gentlemen?" Edward asked with a smug grin.

They turned away and started walking toward Edward's office, leaving the dumbfounded agents behind, but not before Christian relayed one more bit of information to CB to communicate with them, which he communicated promptly.

"Hey guys... Feel free to give me a call if you want to talk about those prehensile tails." He looked back at Dr. Asher whispering, "What the hell is a prehensile tail?"

"Very impressive! I loved the look on their faces, especially after the prehensile tail comment," Edward snickered.

"Just a little something Christian told me," CB smiled.

No sooner than the door to his office was closed Edward blurted, "What the hell are you doing here? I thought you left a half hour ago before all this went down."

CB knew he couldn't tell Edward why Christian came back. It would crush him, the thought of his son killing another, especially one who was completely defenseless. Avoiding specifics he replied, "I know, I know, we were outside when Christian decided he had to do something else. That's why we came back in. The agents arrived a minute after we did."

"What the hell did he have to do that was so important?" Edward inquired.

CB tensed, "I don't know, he didn't tell me…"

Edward was dumbfounded at why Christian would take such a big chance and asked, "I know it's a silly question, but did you guys cause the…"

"Explosion," CB interrupted, "that was all your son's…"

Edward interrupted, "It had to be, that has Christian written all over it. He used to hide in the ventilation system and listen to conversations through the vents. He thought he was some kind of spy or something. But what the hell was he thinking coming back? He's smarter than that!" he bellowed. CB could only respond with a shrug.

"Where is Christian? Is he OK? I have to talk to him. I have something very important to tell him," Edward asked excitedly.

"He's OK, he's across the street waiting for me to pick him up, but I can't get to the car with all the agents running around. Plus they've got drones circling the building," CB said.

"I know, they've got us locked down tight." Edward continued thinking for a way around the heightened security.

"Can't you do the camera thing with them?" Edward inquired.

CB looked at him with surprise, "How do you know about that?"

"I heard them talking about it, something about whenever Christian is around, cameras go blank or something. Can't you do that?"

"Drones are not like the surveillance systems in buildings. The drones have individual power cells which makes it a whole other ballgame." CB continued to explain that the ability to distort hardwired surveillance was easy, but drones with a zoom lens over three hundred feet away required individual attention, and that it was not easily accomplished without exposing yourself to the cameras first.

"I think I should get out of here now. Any suggestions?" CB asked.

"Don't worry, I'll get you out, but I have to talk to Christian. It's important."

CB hesitated, "There is one way, but I don't know how it will affect you. I haven't done it for a while."

"I don't care... I have to talk to him, it's important," Edward pleaded.

"This may leave you a little fuzzy when it's over, but it should work. Sit here," CB tapped the edge of the desk.

He placed his hands with fingers spread on Edward's forehead making a tactile connection, and focused for a moment to open up a transfer of neural energy between them and simultaneously connected with Christian telepathically.

Edward, apprehensive, watched CB's eyes change, not dark or scary like he'd witnessed with Christian behind the museum, they grew brighter. He stared in awe of this transformation until he felt a surge of energy as the neuro tactile connection fully engaged, flooding him with a flurry of thoughts, thoughts and memories that were not his own, but shared with CB and Christian.

"What's up?" Christian asked.

"Your father's going to help me get out, but he had something important he wanted to tell you himself. He's connected."

Edward's eyes were pinned wide open as the surge of neural energy passed into him. He gasped with exhilaration at the wonders he could see through the lifetimes of memories he was now sharing.

"Wow, I'm lightheaded," he thought, unknowingly sharing his thoughts with them.

"Calm down Dad, calm down," Christian urged.

Edward gathered himself as the rush of Christian and CB's thoughts continued to race through his mind.

"OK, OK, I will," he panted. "This is absolutely amazing, I can hear you both, without saying a word. Where are you?"

"Pretty freaky, huh Dad?" Christian inquired in a subdued tone.

"To say the least," Edward replied, continuing without speaking a word. "Christian I have to tell you something you're not going to b-e-l-i-e-v-e..."

Edward jumped, startled by the office door flying open just as he was going to share the incredible news. CB quickly broke off the connection and grabbed Edward as his eyes rolled back, knowing well he'd have little strength to support himself.

"GET OUT," CB yelled at the young agent standing in the doorway. He complied.

The excessive use of neural energy during the connection exhausted Edward's neurotransmitters leaving him with temporary mental and physical fatigue. CB braced him for a while longer, waiting for him to reboot so to speak. "Great, now I remember why I don't do this often," he said aloud, still supporting Edward.

The connection and transfer of external neural energy has such a dramatic effect on people not used to the experience. Dazed and still a bit unsteady, Edward called the agent in. CB bought him some extra time to recuperate by feigning an examination of his eyes. The agent entered.

"It's normal for you to feel a little fuzzy for a few minutes as the medication takes effect," CB explained fictitiously.

He turned to look at the agent who was watching closely.

"We'll be with you in a moment." Turning back to Edward, "How you feeling?"

"Better thanks," Edward replied, clearly fatigued and still a little dizzy.

CB continued, feigning his consultation, "Well, either way, you should see my ophthalmologist to rule out any other issues. I'll send him a text and let him know you'll be calling over the next day or two."

CB turned his attention to the agent standing in the doorway, "What can we do for you?"

"Is he OK?" the agent inquired.

"Yes, he'll be fine. How can we help you?" CB replied.

"Dr. Asher, you need to come quick. They said to bring Dr. Channa... Channa-something with you if he was still around. Is that you?" he asked looking at CB.

CB nodded affirmatively and released his hold on Edward.

Edward, still a bit wobbly, glanced at CB and back to the agent, "What's this about?"

"It's a miracle," the agent said with guarded elation.

"What do you mean it's a miracle?" Edward asked nervously. "How could they have found her already?" he wondered with a concerned look on his face.

It's like nothing ever happened. How'd you do it? They want you to come right away," insisted the agent with subdued excitement.

"Where is she?" Edward asked.

"She? I'm talking about Morano. Who are you talking about?" the agent questioned.

"Sorry, my mistake. I meant where is he? I must still be a little fuzzy from the ocular anesthetic Dr. Channarong applied."

"How could this be possible?" he wondered. He glanced back

at CB who had an odd look on his face; it was a combination of happiness, relief and curiosity.

CB was happy that his friend had made the right choice, but how is possible that Morano was now OK? Christian was far from possessing healing abilities.

Clearing his throat to get CB's attention, "Do you know anything about this Dr. C.?"

"Oh yes, yes..." CB stumbled, "Dr. Williamson and I paid him a visit earlier today. I'm happy to say the new therapy you employed is working wonders. It's almost like a miracle... remarkable progress. I'll have the nurse get you the update and have a copy of the report sent over to you as soon as it is transcribed," CB replied moving toward the door.

Edward caught on quickly; Williamson was Christian's name prior to his adoption by the Asher's.

CB looked at the agent as he passed into the hallway. "Dr. Asher is the attending on this case. Your friend is in the best hands possible."

Edward was a bit confused and unsure how someone in a medically induced coma could just wake up, but after witnessing Amy's miraculous reanimation he had no doubt of its possibility. He followed CB into the hallway hoping to learn more about the incredibly effective treatment responsible for Morano's recovery, "Yes, I'd like to see that report."

He glanced at the agent, "Tell them I'll be up in a minute."

The agent started to speak. "But they said to..."

"I know what they said. Tell them I'll be up in a minute," he insisted.

"I'll walk you out," Edward said, hoping to share the exciting news about Amy with CB. Noticing the agent was on their heels and listening closely, he decided he best wait to share the news. "Give my best to Dr. Williamson and make sure to stay in touch," Edward assertively suggested as they made their way to the lobby. "I still need to speak with him on that other matter... It's important."

"I'll make sure of it," CB smiled, thanking him for the escort as he headed out the front door toward the car. He could feel the agent's eyes on the back of his head, following every step he made. By the time he reached the car the drones were again being released from the surveillance van barely fifty feet from where he was parked. He kept his head down as they passed over, hiding his face from view as he climbed into the car.

Minutes after her arrival, Pamela Kearns was summoned to the fifth floor. Entering Morano's room she was taken aback to find he was no longer in a medically induced coma. Instead, he was sitting up chatting with the other agents on scene as if nothing had ever happened to him. The agents snapped back as Kearns entered the room.

"Is someone going to tell me what's going on here?" she demanded.

"You missed him, he was here about fifteen minutes ago," Morano said, unable to restrain the smile on his face.

"Who was here?" Kearns inquired sternly.

"The kid... you know the kid from New Year's. He was here," Morano replied.

"Was he alone?" she asked.

"Yes, ma'am."

"You're sure of that?"

"Yes ma'am, as far as I know he was the only one here."

"Tell me everything that happened," Kearns again demanded.

"It was all so strange... like a bad dream that turned into a nightmare."

"Nightmare?" Kearns looked on with doubt as the smile dropped from Morano's face and he began to explain.

"Ever since that night, you know, the night it happened, I have relived that night, over and over again as if it just happened. I can feel the excitement of the chase, and all of the action at the scene the moment he gave up. Adrenalin was surging through me, my heart was pounding. I was filled with nervous excitement, this being the first real chase I had ever been involved with. My sites were on him as he was cuffed, then I felt it fire... I didn't want to shoot, it just went off. God knows I didn't want to, but it was too late. I smelled the gases released from the cartridge as I watched the dart fly through the air. I've seen it a thousand times since that night... watching it all, over and over in slow motion as the dart flew through the air toward the kid," he paused, taking a deep mournful breath, "...and then I see her. In my dreams I tried to yell to her, but I was too late."

"I watched as the dart pierced her skull. I could hear the bone crack and see the gush of blood shooting from the wound splattering everything around her, including him. He looked right at me, and then... and then his face changed." Morano shivered.

"I could see his rage. The next thing I heard was this ungodly scream coming from him as he ripped his arms apart, shattering his cuffs and dropping low trying to catch her body before she hit the ground. I watched as she fell limp in his arms with him kneeling by her side, caressing her bloody hair and then he roared again."

Morano trembled, "That's a sound I will never forget... it was unearthly. It was agony, heartbreak and rage. I knew I had crushed his very soul the second I heard it. Some of the others must have heard it too." He glanced around the room at the other agents listening to his tale, but non dare admit to the frightening facts.

"I watched, frozen with fear as his eyes turned black and lifeless, like death itself was staring at me." He fumbled his words, "I didn't think I could be more scared, but I was wrong. As he walked toward me his cold, dark eyes started to glow with an eerie blue iridescence and then fire... like the fires of hell.

"Go on," Kearns urged.

"I tried to run, but I couldn't move as he approached. Her blood was splattered all over him and dripping from his hands. I could see the torment in his face as he raised his arms and blasted every agent around me with some type of incredibly powerful pulse."

"The pulse... tell me about the pulse. We didn't find a weapon, so where did the pulse come from? Was it a small EMP device of some kind? What did he use?"

"No, nothing like that. It was some type of energy pulse, like a shock wave from an explosion. I couldn't see how he did it, all I know is he was able to somehow direct it away from me and target the other agents, taking them out. The second blast was only similar in that it came out of him too."

"What do you mean, 'came out of him'?" Kearns questioned.

"Whatever it was or is, it came out of his body... like some type of energy he built up and stored inside himself and then released."

"Where did this energy come from? Was there a power source of some kind?" Kearns asked.

"No, not that I saw. I remember something strange happened just before it shot out of him. I heard a crackling sound like static electricity and the air and ground around him appeared distorted, wavy, like a mirage you see on the roadway on really hot days. It sounds crazy but it looked like he was absorbing energy from everything around him."

Kearns looked on in disbelief thinking, "What am I missing here? There's nothing like this in any of the reports."

She was referring to her former mentor, the late Dr. Stedwell's reports. She had read them all many times over. In her haste to assume control of his research she overlooked one thing; the possibility that he may have had more than one storage facility for his many years of research on the original fourteen, the fraternity of equally gifted men and women from 1964.

Stedwell loved his research and documented the full spectrum of the abilities shared by the fourteen, but he knew well that his research would end if he were to report all he had learned over the years. The government would shut him down and lock up the fourteen for their amazing abilities and he couldn't let that happen, so he kept more than one set of books and researched his people in the field away from home base for privacy. This allowed him to protect his position by documenting their less threatening powers for the government and protect the few who shared their more dangerous abilities with him from the risk of incarceration or worse, by documenting their abilities far outside of any government facility. He also kept a wary eye out for people just like Pamela Kearns. Unfortunately he was not as diligent with that as he was with his research. His private collection documenting everything he had witnessed, all of their abilities and skills, was hidden carefully. He always said he kept his research in his head, just in case the unimaginable were to happen, and thanks to Kearns, it had.

"I'll bet that old bastard has been hiding the truth about these freaks since his research began," Kearns mumbled under her breath.

Morano shivered, "As he moved toward me I hit him with more tranqs, two I think, but they did nothing. That's when he raised his arm, pointed it in my direction, and shot the car."

"Shot the car… with what? I saw the car flip, but I didn't see anything shoot out of him What did he shoot the car with?" she asked again.

"It's hard to explain."

"Do your best. Was it the same as the pulse that took out the agents?" she questioned impatiently.

"No it was very different. Like I said, the ground and air around him appeared distorted when he pointed his arm, and then a silver blue dart-shaped light shot out of him and blew up the car. That's the last I remember until I looked up to see those lifeless, unforgiving eyes staring down at me."

"Did he say anything?" Kearns asked.

Morano thought for a moment, "Yes, but I don't know what he said."

Kearns looked at him oddly, "What do you mean?" she asked, her curiosity peaked.

"He started to speak, at least I think he was speaking; his lips were moving, but it wasn't anything I've ever heard before. It was guttural and coarse sounding like growling, but not. I can't explain it."

"And then?" she probed.

"His black eyes started to glow again, slowly at first and then brighter and brighter. I could feel the pressure inside my entire body building. It felt like electricity or some type of energy was passing through me and up into him. I couldn't breathe, everything hurt. My skin felt as if it was being peeled off my body and my muscles pulled to the point I could feel them starting to tear from my bones. Every joint in my body ached. I tried to look away, but I couldn't. As his eyes glowed brighter, the pressure in my head increased until it was unbearable. The last thing I remember are the pictures."

Morano sat exhausted from reliving the tale, his color had paled and he was trembling.

"Pictures?" Kearns asked.

"Yes, pictures of a beautiful girl with soft, light brown hair, sparkling green eyes and a beautiful smile, lying in a pool of blood because of me. Then in front of my eyes her beauty faded as she morphed into some demonic apparition flying toward me with flames for eyes and the shrill of Satan himself. I don't know how, but it seemed as if she was taking part of my soul with each dream, over and over again."

Kearns rolled her eyes. "Let's get back to today. What happened today? Tell me about him. What happened when he came into this room?" Kearns demanded with growing impatience.

"I guess I was laying on my side facing the window; at least that's the position I was in when I woke up. I didn't hear the door open, but I somehow knew someone came into the room. I could feel his presence. I remember trying to open my eyes, but couldn't. My heart was pounding. I thought he was here to finish the job and I prayed that he would. Then I felt the warmth of his hand over my face. He didn't touch me, he just held his hand over my face and somehow I was able to open my eyes. My thoughts were clear and I was free of my living nightmare for the first time in what seemed an eternity. Then I heard him say, 'Thank you Hwei Ru.'"

"Hwei Ru? Sounds like a name. Check it out," she directed one of the agents.

"I made my peace with God, thinking he was going to kill me, then he changed."

"Changed?" Kearns questioned.

"I thought I was dreaming, but I wasn't. His eyes, face... everything changed. The last thing I remember was the brightest light I had ever seen. I strained to keep my eyes open but couldn't. I wasn't nervous anymore, I felt peaceful and warm." Morano laughed softly remembering, "I thought it was heaven. Next thing you know I was up and talking with you guys," he smiled thankfully.

Morano was cognizant of the fact that Christian, for whatever reason, had spared him from the agony he had endured since New Year's Eve. He couldn't understand why though, especially now that he had learned from the other agents that Amy had died this very same day as a result of his actions. That made it all the more strange to him, and although his allegiance was to the United States government, he felt grateful and somehow indebted to Christian for his redemption.

"Where did he go?" Kearns asked.

"I don't know, the last thing I remember is the light," he replied. "When I opened my eyes, he was gone and you guys were here."

"Is there anything else?" Kearns asked.

"No, nothing."

Kearns looked at the agent standing beside her. "Pack him up. I want him in Langley by the end of the day. He's on twenty-four seven until I'm finished with him. Call Dr. Crimi. I want him tested for everything. Things like this just don't happen..." Kearns turned and hurried out the door.

Kearns left the room and headed for the elevator. Her cell rang and she stepped into the empty sitting room to take a brief call. As she looked out the window something caught her eye; it was someone getting into a car. "What was it about this guy?"

was the question that gnawed at her mind. Finishing her call she headed downstairs, ordering Davenport to meet her in the lobby. He met her at the elevator. "Where's Asher?" she asked.

"He's on his way to the fifth floor to check out Morano," Davenport replied.

"Did you question him?"

"Yes."

"What did he say?" Kearns asked continuing, "Let me guess... he didn't see his son, right?"

"Yes ma'am, that's exactly what he said."

"Follow me and have your two monkeys keep an eye on him. I don't want him slipping away from us."

Kearns led Davenport to security. As she entered, the security officer was ordered to play the footage from the last hour of video surveillance. "There it is. What time did the video go bad?" she asked the security guard.

"I've never seen anything like it, this is the third time it happened today," he responded.

"What do you mean the third time today? Show me everything," she ordered with her usual demanding tone.

"A little more than an hour and a half ago everything went blank; outside first then inside. Then thirty-five minutes later the inside surveillance returned for a minute or two then went out again... Damnedest thing I've ever seen."

"When did it come back on again?" she questioned.

"About fifteen to twenty minutes later, just about the time you guys arrived, but only the inside came on," the security officer replied.

"You said three times. When was the third?"

"Twenty to twenty-five minutes ago the inside went out again, and cleared up just before you walked in."

Kearns looked at Davenport, "He's close. Not only was he here, I'll bet my life on it that the good doctor and his son had a nice long chat when he came to see his girlfriend. Where is the little bitch?" she demanded.

"She's dead ma'am. According to the doctors we questioned, they pulled the plug about twenty minutes after the videos went out."

"Did you verify that?" Kearns asked.

"Yes ma'am. Tully was just down there, she was gone."

"You're sure about that? Would you bet your job on it, because you just might be," she sneered.

"Yes ma'am. Here's a pic he took with his phone. He sent it to me with his confirmation."

"OK, but he came back for a reason, and if he can fix that brain-dead lump of crap Morano, then he may be able to do the same for her. Check it again," she ordered.

"Yes ma'am." As Davenport walked away he paused to ask, "And the Dr.?"

"He's pulled my strings for the last time. Wrap him up, he's coming with us too. It's time we had a nice long chat with him. Maybe our friend Dr. Crimi can help with him too," she said with a sinister grin.

"Yes ma'am!" Davenport said, enthused with the idea of using Dr. Crimi's unusual services.

Kearns returned to the command post. "Show me the drone surveillance. Now." She was surprised to see there was actual footage. No sooner did she start to watch the videos, she caught a glimpse of a man entering the back of the hospital. This sparked her interest even further. "Who is this guy? What time was this?"

"About twenty-five minutes ago ma'am."

She continued to review at speed until the end and switched to the live feed to review the last few minutes. Her eye was keen picking up on CB again, this time walking up to the car. It was only a few seconds but it drew her attention. "When was this?" she barked.

"A few minutes, give or take." She turned to the surveillance team, "Find out where this guy came from and give me a live scan of the entire area, now! Also, match him going into and out of the hospital with security footage. Let's see if he's our guy..."

Davenport interrupted, "Ma'am, the packages are wrapped and ready for delivery."

"Move them out and make the good doctor feel at home." That was her way of saying, put him in the steel box she called a surveillance room upon their arrival at home base. "And throw Morano in there with him."

"Morano, ma'am? But he's one of us" he questioned.

"Just do it! You got a problem with that?" she barked.

"No ma'am, consider it done." Davenport turned to head back to his car.

Her eyes sparkled and a rare smile appeared on her face. "Hold it, I might need you for something else. Get someone else to escort our guests."

"Yes ma'am," Davenport replied and proceeded to his car, arranging for another agent to take the packages to the airport for transport to home base in Langley.

"Rewind that. Play it back... stop there. Zoom in on him," she pointed to the screen. The tech zoomed in on the man getting into the car. Her excitement grew.

"How long ago was this?"

"A few minutes tops, ma'am."

"Gotcha you SOB! Where's that live feed? I want to see where this car went, NOW," she barked.

Kearns' talent was her attention to detail. While reviewing the video feed she came across the one thing that could identify CB, a split second shot of his foot when he stepped into the car sporting his purple Nike's.

The tech chimed in, "Got him. He's driving north along the east side of the hospital.

Kearns clicked on her radio, "Davenport, the suspect's car is a blue, early model Monte Carlo travelling north on the service road east of the hospital. Tail him, but do not pursue until I give the order. Don't screw this up."

"Yes ma'am." Davenport started his cruiser.

He hit the gas and raced out of the lot with Kearns still barking orders over the radio. Anticipating what would happen next, she ordered her traps set. "He's going to pick him up. Block all intersections north and east." Agency cruisers raced out of the hospital lots in every direction.

She watched the live feed anxiously until she saw what she was praying for. CB pulled over to the side of the road.

"There!" she barked, "Zoom in on him now," and there he was, her prize. Christian came running out from under the tree line and dove into the car.

"GO, GO, GO..." blared over the agent's radios as Kearns ordered her attack.

Edward and Morano, on their way to East Hampton Airport for their trip back to home base next to Langley, listened intently as agency cruisers closed in on their prey.

"Looks like you'll be reunited with your son before you know it, hey Doc?" an agent smirked.

"Phew! That was close. If it wasn't for your father, well you know..." said CB relieved. "He saved my butt. I can't believe you ever doubted him."

Christian jumped in, "Yeah, me either, but right now we have something else to worry about." Christian pointed to the next intersection rapidly filling with agency cruisers.

"And they have friends," CB said, watching cruisers gaining from behind.

"Great!" he said sarcastically, "I wish you were driving."

"Me too," Christian added nervously.

Waiting at the intersection were a half a dozen agency cars. The police were on alert, standby only, and blocking all alternate routes of escape. Kearns wanted this to be an agency-only apprehension.

CB readied himself, "Man, I wish this thing had a shoulder strap," he said as he pulled the lap belt across his waist and locked it in, glancing at Christian.

"Ready? Let's do this." He hit the gas and spun the car around, with tires screaming, the chase was on. The smell of burnt rubber and smoke filled the roadway. Christian, familiar with the area, helped CB negotiate the roadways, allowing them to temporarily lose their pursuers in the quiet neighborhood streets, but that wasn't enough. Radios and air support covering the chase were more than enough to allow the agency to set the next trap for their prey.

With tension building, the pair made it to a tree lined main roadway and raced north to their intended escape route. Christian watched closely as they approached the small cluster of businesses and buildings that occupied the area adjacent to the highway.

"Something's not right…" Christian said, craning around and seeing that they were alone.

"Yeah, it's too quiet. Keep your eyes open," CB said. "They're around somewhere I can feel it."

"Get ready," CB said. "See those guys, and those guys, and them?" he pointed to three separate locations. "Unless there's a funeral parlor around here, that's way too many suits for this area."

"What are they up to?" Christian asked a second too soon.

B-A-M! His head hit the side window as the Monte took a hit in the passenger rear. CB controlled the impact forced skid, an over-eager agent's failed attempt to do a pit maneuver.

"Where the hell did that come from?" CB shouted, hitting the gas.

The well-hidden agency cars poured out from every direction, blocking all escape routes, especially the parkway entrance. Christian reacted quickly, pulling the steering wheel to the right, "Turn here NOW!"

CB turned hard into a construction staging area being used for ongoing repairs to the roadway.

"I have an idea… head to the back," Christian pointed. The large staging area had its own fenced off entrance to the highway.

"We got you now," Davenport smiled confidently, squinting to see through the wall of dust.

CB swerved wildly, kicking up clouds of dust and pelting agency cars with tiny stones as he made his way to the back of the site and blasted through the fence leading to the highway.

"Yes!" CB claimed his small victory as they hit the highway.

"A little premature for celebration, don't you think?" Christian asked, pointing to a swarm of agency cars pouring out of the massive dust cloud that covered the roadway behind them.

"What the... how can there be more of them?" CB questioned, looking back at a line of well over a dozen units now chasing them. He raced eastbound until he found his spot, a muddy turn-around the DOT trucks used. The concrete dividers were partially closed off for some reason. It didn't take long to discover why.

He swung the Chevy right, then left, and locked his brakes, skidding to align himself with the narrow opening. Hitting the gas hard he headed straight for the concrete dividers. Christian cringed, leaned in toward the middle of the car and braced himself.

"This is going to be tight," he said, glancing at CB once more. "What the hell are you doing? Open your eyes!" he yelled as the car squeezed through the barriers.

The Monte blasted through a muddy pond formed by a recent snow melt with mere inches to spare on either side.

"Open your E-Y-E-S!!!" Christian yelled again.

"Woo Hoo!!! We made it!" CB celebrated and hit the brakes, turning hard left.

"Phew," Christian sighed, relieved they had made it through, but his stomach had different feelings. It was rumbling like Mount Vesuvius as CB hit the gas heading west.

It was only moments before CB heard, "Oh no... " from his passenger who was staring ahead.

"What now... you going to chuck your cookies?" he asked, grinning.

"Look up there," Christian pointed.

"What am I looking at?" CB asked.

"Nothing!" Christian pointed further up the roadway to the bridge... there was none! The construction crews renovating the bridge had removed the roadway surface from the overpass, leaving a seventy-five foot section of open roadway.

"Oh, this just keeps getting better and better," CB said, pointing back.

The agents had found another turn around and were pushing their cruisers hard to close the gap between them. Thinking quick, CB swerved right and slid the car down the muddy grass embankment and onto the service road. The car fishtailed wildly, throwing clumps of grass, mud and small stones into the air as the tires spun trying to regain a firm grip on the road. As they sped west they could see agency cars forming a gauntlet in the intersection ahead of them. Agents taking positions behind their cruisers drew down on the Monte.

"You thinking what I'm thinking?" asked CB, calculating.

"I hope not," Christian responded with concerned curiosity. "Hey, do me a favor... Keep your eyes open this time!" Christian forced a nervous laugh, nauseated at the thought of what was to come.

CB pushed the pedal to the floor. The barrels opened up on the LS5 454 ci Mark IV engine and the Monte took off. Increasingly nervous agents watched as the speeding Monte barreled toward the intersection with no sign of letting up.

"What the hell does he think he's doing?" Davenport asked, standing next to one of the cruisers. All but a few agents began to scatter. "That crazy bastard, he's going to try and jump it!" Davenport ran to his cruiser hidden under the overpass ready to pursue.

CB fixed his focus on the agents as the Monte screamed down the roadway. Just as he saw the panic in their eyes he swerved left, flying up the side of the embankment and launched the Monte into the air. The rocky launch unnerving them both.

"Oh... O-H... O-H-H-H-H-H-H... S-H-I-I-I-I-T!!!!" they yelled simultaneously as the Monte launched itself off the grassy ramp. Christian's face paled as he spewed out the window and onto the agents cowering below. BAM! The Monte slammed down with a painful crash, the rear tires landing only inches from the edge of the open overpass.

"Phew! Cutting kind of close, don't you think?" Christian asked holding his stomach and looking a bit green. "At least you kept your eyes open this time," he said, 'vurping', a distasteful vomit burp.

The forceful impact dislodged the rear bumper, breaking it free of the car. Bouncing off the edge of the roadway it flipped wildly through the air before falling through the open roadway and crashing through the windshield of an occupied agency cruiser – Davenport's cruiser.

The startled agents jumped nervously from the impact.

"Son of a... what's with this kid? He's always messing up my cars!" the driver said, looking over at Davenport who sat quietly, frozen in place with both hands firmly grasping his crotch. A cold sweat beaded on his forehead as the stinging between his legs turned to a warm numb sensation. His lips started to tremble and then he slowly began to speak.

"A... A... Are they still there?" he stuttered nervously.

The agent wasted no time with his spiteful reply. "No, it looks like they jumped clear across," he said, knowing all too well that Davenport was not asking about the car making the jump.

"NOT THE CAR YOU IDIOT, MY BALLS... ARE THEY STILL THERE?" a very nervous Davenport yelled.

The agent enjoyed this rare opportunity to mess with Davenport. He had always been a power hungry pain in the butt who would do anything to get ahead. The driver looked down, restraining his urge to laugh. There was no blood. The only casualty was Davenport's pants which were badly torn, the front now resembling a tent flap with a zipper.

"You're fine," he smirked, "Take your hand off your balls and look for yourself," he said as he hopped out of the car, leaving Davenport to fend for himself.

Still in shock with his mouth wide open and nervously gasping for air, Davenport slowly peeled his hands away from his crotch. "Oh thank you, thank you, thank you," he praised, seeing his goodies were still with him.

The bumper had pierced through the seat and was lodged up against his groin. Other than having a few wide scratches on the inside of each thigh and badly torn pants, he was fine. His shock turned to relief and then to anger. He reached for the radio mic to connect with the agents in pursuit.

"Son of a bitch!" Davenport slammed the broken mic down and awkwardly extricated himself from behind the bumper-turned-projectile. His anger was more apparent than ever as he stormed across the street to a group of snickering agents who were already aware of what had transpired.

"What's so funny?" Davenport barked as he approached.

"Oh nothing..." a few brave souls replied, straining not to laugh as Davenport approached them with the crotch of his pants flapping in the wind.

He had stepped on many of them in his attempts to climb the ranks and most of them believed the world would be a much better place if he had actually lost his ability to reproduce.

"Who's on them? I want to talk to them now," he demanded. He was directed to another agency cruiser. As he stormed over to the cruiser, one of the agents couldn't resist, "Sir, I think your fly is open." The gaggle of them burst out laughing.

"Very funny... assholes," an embarrassed Davenport growled

angrily. Reaching agent Sanderson's cruiser, Davenport threw open the door and yanked him out of the car and hopped in to monitor the chase.

The now displaced Sanderson stepped into the cluster of nearby agents and murmured, "Where's a bumper when you need one?" The agents again burst out laughing.

Davenport clicked in on the mic. "What's your twenty?" he shouted. The radio fell silent. "What's your twenty?" he shouted again, impatiently waiting for a response.

"Sir, suspects are westbound on 27. We have visual and anticipate intercept in 2 minutes."

"Don't lose them and keep me posted. I'm on my way," Davenport ordered.

He hopped out of the car barking orders to the agents on site, "Secure the scene." The remaining agents strained not to laugh in his face but lost it when a comment was tossed his way by someone in the crowd of curious onlookers. Davenport boiled, "Get your asses out of here, NOW!" he ordered.

"But sir, what about the roadway?"

"Forget it! The locals can handle it. Move out...Now!"

Davenport, embarrassed, humiliated and angry, stormed back to his car and grabbed hold of the bumper and tried to rip it from the windshield without success. He threw his hands up in frustration, kicked the car and turned to the snickering driver, "Take your ass and this piece of crap back to command."

His crotch flap swinging in the wind, he made his way across the street and pulled another agent out of his car. "You go with him," he ordered, jumping into the cruiser and speeding away, determined to be in on the capture.

Christian gulped down the chyme that had climbed up to the back of his throat. "That was amazing... scary as all hell, but amazing. How did you calculate how fast to go to clear the opening in the bridge?"

"Easy! I took the minimum width of the lanes at twelve feet, times four, and center median at four feet. A little multiplication and addition and I came up with fifty-two feet. Based on the weight of the car plus two people and one hundred pounds for miscellaneous items and the estimated angle of our grassy launch ramp, I figured out how fast we should go to make it across the bridge," CB smiled almost arrogantly.

Christian swallowed hard again, trying to hold back the vomit. "Really, didn't you forget something... what about the shoulders, wouldn't that make it closer to seventy feet?" Christian said waiting for his response.

CB paused in thought, his lips moving as he recalculated the numbers, "Oh, I guess we got lucky then," he smirked.

– Four –
The Flying Wasp

D avenport listened anxiously to the action playing out over the radio. He sped recklessly toward the reported location of the chase while remaining in constant contact with the team of pursuing agents both in the air and on the ground. His confidence swelled as thoughts of the promotion that would surely come from this arrest played out in his mind. He smiled at the thought.

"What the hell is that…?"

Davenport's confidence wilted at the tone of the pilot's voice. "What the hell is what?" he demanded to know.

"Sir, I thought this area was cleared of all air traffic?" the pilot questioned.

"It is, what's happening?"

"Well someone didn't tell this guy," the pilot added, attempting to hail the unmarked aircraft. "You are in restricted airspace. Vacate the vicinity immediately." There was no response.

"What the hell are you doing?" he wondered, keeping one eye on the car and the other on the inbound helicopter, a Sikorsky CH-54 Tarhe or, as he liked to call it, the flying wasp.

"I repeat, this is restricted airspace. Leave the area immediately." The approaching aircraft continued to ignore the calls, flying directly toward the pursuit.

Cold and focused, the unidentified pilot flipped an arming switch and locked onto the pursuit chopper. Squeezing the trigger he released an invisible pulse. "Bye-Bye," he murmured with a sinister grin.

The pursuit copter shuddered as it lost power, the console sparking and popping, filling the cabin with smoke. "God damn it, what the hell is going on here?" the pilot questioned, assessing the damage. "Civilians don't have EMP devices!"

Acting quickly he pitched the nose up to use the remaining energy of the main rotors to slow his descent.

"What's happening?" Davenport demanded to know, looking ahead at the pursuit helicopter as it dropped quickly from the sky. His attempts to call were unheard.

"What the hell is he doing?" CB asked, catching a glimpse of the rapidly dropping helicopter.

"It looks like he's – CRASHING! DUCK!" Christian shouted seconds before the tail rotor ripped through the top of the Monte, showering them with debris.

"Jesus Christ!" Christian yelled, craning to watch the chopper hit the roadway with a loud crash behind them. Its skids partially collapsed, the pursuit copter spewed a shower of sparks as it screeched loudly, skidding toward an oncoming fuel truck.

Taking evasive action, the truck driver hit the brakes hard and swerved left to avoid the wildly skidding chopper ahead in the roadway. The rear brakes locked, causing the half full trailer to chatter and swing sideways. Gaining momentum, the container bounced and twisted violently, breaking free of the tractor cab and flipping end over end. Gas spewed from broken valves at the rear of the container. Vapor trails and gaseous mist filled the air crossing the roadway.

The veteran pilot's eyes widened. Was he to suffer an airmen's worst nightmare, an agonizing death by fire. He watched helplessly as the uncontrolled trailer drew closer, but his luck would hold out this day – or would it?

Seconds before impact, the valves on the back of the container hit the center divider, slowing the trailer's momentum. The container swung right and slammed into the center divider, allowing the chopper to pass within feet of the spewing container. But luck is a fickle thing.

The chopper slid through the vapor trail, igniting the airborne mist, and in a flash the container was in flames. The pilot jumped from the cockpit and ran for cover. Abandoned cars littered both sides of the roadway as motorists fled the scene. What seemed like minutes was only seconds as the fire took its prize, triggering a massive explosion of the container that could be seen for miles.

The pursuing agents broadcast the events while skillfully evading the action unfolding in front of them. "Chopper down, chopper down!" they yelled, "Oh my god! Look out, LOOK O-U-T!" The radio fell silent.

Davenport listened anxiously to the agent's calls and the massive explosion that followed. "Damn it!" He looked ahead to see a ball of flame shooting hundreds of feet into the air. "Son of a bitch!" He pounded the steering wheel in frustration, pushing his cruiser to reach the scene. He slammed on the cruiser's brakes, skidding to a stop and jumped from the car. He surveyed the devastation while working his way through the debris lying across the smoke-filled roadway.

Dr. Asher, Morano and a crew of three agents had just taken off from East Hampton Airport aboard one of the company's infamous unmarked black jets. As the pilot turned southwest toward Langley, Edward witnessed the explosion off in the distance. He watched anxiously as the plume of smoke and flames mushroomed into the sky. Feeling helpless and uncertain as to the terrible fate that may have befallen his son, he watched the plume grow smaller and smaller as the jet made its way further south. All he could do was pray that if it was Christian, somehow he and CB had escaped harm. He turned away from the window and looked into the eyes of a surprisingly sympathetic Morano who softly whispered, "Don't worry about him, he'll be just fine."

"Thank you," Edward said, wishing he could be as optimistic as Agent Morano.

Katheryn and the Kendalls were at the beach house warming up with a cup of coffee, unaware of all that had transpired since Edward asked them to leave the hospital. Katheryn tried to explain to them why the military and other government agencies were involved and why Edward had asked them to leave without disclosing any of the particulars. She knew well that the less they knew, the better off they would be, but John Kendall was well aware that there was more to it than Katheryn was letting on.

Katheryn started to pace, her intuition kicking in, making her head ache. It was the kind of pain she had whenever something was not right. She picked up her phone to call Edward at the hospital, but second guessed her decision, thinking agency personnel would still be actively searching the hospital and grounds. Taking a break from the conversation she turned on the television.

She flipped through the channels finding reporter after reporter talking about the breaking news story. The news of the dramatic chase had spread like wildfire. Just about every channel was covering it. Reporters were interviewing witnesses and showing footage of the chase, including the helicopter pursuit which was being played over and over again by every station.

"What is going on now?" she thought, praying this didn't have anything to do with Christian and Edward. "Who am I kidding? Of course it has to do with them."

As luck would have it, one TV crew was a mile or two behind the chase. Their timing couldn't have been better as they arrived on scene to witness the explosive conclusion.

Pulling up to the devastation, the crew wasted no time broadcasting the story live. One reporter already in the middle of his report described, "As I said, what actually happened here appears to have been a chain reaction. It's a miracle no one was killed. This eyewitness states that he saw a blue Monte Carlo being chased by one of these charred sedans behind me. He recorded most of it with this cell phone," the reporter held the man's phone tight to his face for the close up, showing it to the camera.

"Sir, can you tell us what happened?" he asked the heavy set man in sweats.

"Yeah, I was on my way home from the gym and I was on the overpass when I saw this black helicopter flying low. It looked like it was chasing a blue Monte Carlo, you know, an old one... 1970's, I think. So I started to record the chase and then just after they flew over my head, the helicopter started falling. I got it all on my phone," he boasted.

Katheryn's heart raced as she watched the footage of the helicopter dropping from the sky and nearly splitting the blue Monte Carlo in two with its tail rotor. "Oh my god! Can't I be wrong just once?" she thought, the strain of worry showing on her face.

"That's Connor's car! What in the world is he doing?" she mumbled to herself.

The witness's next statement cinched it. "Then these men-in-black-type guys came out and took everyone's phones and tried to chase us away." The man smiled.

The reporter again held the man's phone next to his face in front of the camera to ensure his close up. "So, sir, tell me, how is that you were able to prevent these "mysterious men" from confiscating your phone and this remarkable footage?"

"Oh, that was easy. I shoved it way down in the back of my pants so they wouldn't find it," the man replied with a victorious smile and doing a little happy dance.

Mr. Kendall burst out laughing watching the reporter's face morph from excitement to nausea as he peeled the phone from his face and handed it back to its portly owner.

It was a tension breaking laugh for him and Debra. Katheryn forced a little laugh to keep up appearances.

The doorbell rang. "Now what?" Katheryn cringed. Opening the door her heart sunk when she saw Connor standing in front of her. "Hi Mrs. Asher! We saw the cars here and thought we'd stop by. Are you OK?" he inquired, noticing Katheryn was out of sorts.

"Not really," Katheryn responded, motioning for him to come into the living room. "Where's Chris?" she asked.

"Oh, he's just finishing up a call with Maddy, he'll be in in a minute," Connor smiled.

"Connor, don't you have an old blue Monte Carlo that you've been working on?"

"Yes!" Connor said proudly, "I finished working on it a couple of months ago. It just got painted," he smiled.

"And would you have possibly loaned that car to anyone today?" she inquired.

"Well... well... I," Connor stuttered, not knowing how to respond.

"That's what I thought..."she said nervously.

"Come over here," Katheryn motioned for him to move in front of the living room television. "Is this your car?" she asked, pointing to the screen.

Connor's face dropped as the chase footage replayed on the screen. "It could be, but where's my bumper?" he asked nervously, assessing the car on the replay.

"You better brace yourself honey," she whispered.

Connor looked at her with confusion as Tweet came through the door and hurried to the living room.

"Oh my god! Is that...?" he asked with a panicked look on his face.

Katheryn hushed him. "Did you happen to see anyone special today?" she asked again.

Christopher hesitated at first, "Yes," but before he could finish he heard his friend yell loudly.

"NO!" cried Connor, grasping his head with both hands as he watched the tail rotor spit open the top of his car.

Giving Connor a comforting hug Katheryn suggested, "I think you boys should leave now. And Connor, when they come asking questions, and they will, you best not tell them that you saw Christian. Tell them Christian knew where you kept the keys. Tell them anything but the fact that you saw him.

Katheryn explained to an inconsolable and now very nervous Connor what the results of his kindness would bring and how he should handle it, if he chose to. She knew the agency would track him down as being the car's owner. She told him they might even take him into custody for questioning. Little did they know, her advice would be helpful within the hour. The boys left and headed for home with Connor mumbling, "But they said they were only going to the hospital..." he whimpered.

Returning to the kitchen Mr. Kendall looked at Katheryn, "I appreciate you trying to spare us, and I know I was born at night, but it wasn't last night. Do you want to tell me what the hell is going on and why these people are chasing your son?"

Katheryn apologized for her avoidance of the topic and explained, however reluctantly, to the Kendall's the special circumstances that surrounded Christian and why she tried protecting them by withholding the truth. She advised them the importance of not disclosing anything they were about to hear.

"It started fifteen years ago when Christian as a young boy was brought to the hospital where Edward was working. His mother had suffered a severe breakdown following his father's suicide. He had remarkable abilities. He was mature beyond his years and had even helped Edward to calm a frantic accident victim. Noticing just how remarkable he was, Edward called in a friend who was in charge of a program that dealt with gifted people of sorts. Knowing the mother would not be able to care for her son Edward and Dr. Stedwell arranged for us to adopt him."

"Together Edward and Dr. Stedwell secretly tested his abilities and found his brain function to be off the charts. That's when they elected to hide his abilities from the government. Stedwell knew that he would become a guinea pig if they hadn't so he prescribed a medication that he developed to suppress higher brain function. As he grew the prescription was adjusted to keep him at a level close to his peers. That was at least until recently."

"When he left for his third term at Cal Poly, we had our concerns, but being as mature as he was we thought he'd continue taking his medication and all would be fine... but we couldn't have been more wrong," pausing she sighed. "During a camping trip with Amy and a few friends he was attacked by something. A bolt of lightning struck his chest and lifted him off the ground, but not just for a second or two." she paused.

"I think it is better that I show you." Katheryn left the room and came back with a laptop and laid it on the counter and pulled up an encrypted video named awakenings and played it.

The Kendall's were speechless. The video started part way through the event when Matt reached the scene. They watched a bolt of lightning that as if somehow guided had targeted Christian and struck him through the chest and slowly lifted him off the ground. They saw firsthand how whirlwinds developed and surrounded him blocking his friends from reaching him. They jumped when targeted lightning strikes stopped Amy and Matt from reaching the top of the mesa. Debra reacted to the terror she saw in her daughter's eyes as they helped Matt to his feet after being thrown twenty plus feet from a lightning strike. They stared in disbelief at the mysterious shadow warriors that appeared out of nowhere and helped to bring Christian back down to the mesa. Katheryn turned off the video and slid the laptop on a shelf under the counter.

"Holy crap!" said John with a stunned look on his face. Debra quietly wiped a tear from her eye offering a consoling look as Katheryn continued,

"And that's when everything changed. Christian started to develop amazing abilities far beyond what he could do as a child. What we didn't know at the time is that the government knew about him all along. Edward and I suspect someone at the hospital may have mentioned him and they have been monitoring him all along. His roommate Matt actually worked for the government, army intelligence I think... and I believe Amy's roommate was with the NSA." Debra's eyebrows raised.

"Once his abilities started to surface things started to happen. I think he knows everything. He has memories of past lives that come to him, one of them led him to a remarkable treasure called the Ferdinand Cross that Christian and Amy found together, and that's when the trouble started. Not only was our government watching, others were as well. Some with interest in Christian and others who pursued him for the cross." Katheryn wiped a tear from her eye and continued,

"The night Amy got hurt," "New Year's Eve," Debra said. "Yes... she wasn't hit by a truck, she was shot by an agent with a tranquilizer dart. I'm sorry but we couldn't tell you what really happened our phones are tapped, the house is bugged and the agency had men following every move we make."

"I knew those sons of bitches had something to do with it," said John angrily.

Katheryn continued, "They came to this neighborhood during the New Year's show my neighbor has every year. They were going to sneak up through the crowd and try to capture Christian, but things got messy. Christian and Amy got away and met up with friends behind the house. That's where Christian left Amy with friends. They were supposed to take care of her while he tried to get away, but,"

"Amy would have none of that... right?" Debra interrupted knowingly.

"No... she wouldn't. She broke free, scaled that fence," Katheryn pointed to the tall fence bordering the side yard, "and dived into the front seat and they were off. Eventually things got out of hand. There were cars and helicopters everywhere and Christian stopped. He couldn't bear to see anything happen to Amy so he gave up."

"So how the hell did she get shot?" John asked angrily.

"They had taken Christian into custody and handcuffed him when one of the agents started to slam Christian's head onto the hood of the car. Amy broke free and ran to help him, that's when the dart hit her."

"What happened to the bastard that shot her... nothing I suppose," asked John.

"Oh no, quite the contrary. Christian hurt him badly, put him in the hospital," Katheryn replied.

"Good, at least I have that satisfaction," mumbled John.

Katheryn continued, "And that's what brought us together today. Christian escaped and came straight here to see Amy and the bastards tracked him here. I guess that's why Edward wanted to hide Amy... to protect her from the agency. If she turned up alive and well they might think she has the same abilities as Christian has and they would take her as well.

"Thank you for sharing this with us. I can understand how hard this is for you," Debra smiled with an accepting look on her face.

"Well I'll be damned. It is true then," said John.

"Excuse me?" Katheryn asked.

"Well I'll be damned twice." He recalled his earlier years, "I grew up with someone who could do the most amazing things. One day he was dumber than a cucumber and the next day he was 'Einstein'. He seemed to know everything overnight. He spoke just about every language there was and could solve any puzzle, math equation or answer any question we tossed at him. His name was Arnold. That SOB could do anything," he reflected. "We joined the military together. He saved our butts more than once until they came and took him away." He paused, thinking of his friend fondly. "Never saw him again."

"Who took him away?" Katheryn asked.

"Suits!" John said, "The only difference is the suits back then were dark grey, not black, but they were the same cold hearted bastards that were there today. They were headed up by a Captain Stedwell. I don't know how he got mixed up with them. He seemed a nice enough guy, even had manners, unlike those other spooks."

Katheryn's eyes widened when John mentioned Stedwell's name. John's description was on the money; Stedwell was a nice man who was interested in the scientific side of what had happened to these men and women.

Seeing Katheryn's response to the name he inquired, "Didn't I hear you mention him earlier?" She nodded affirmatively without going into detail other than mentioning he was a very nice guy that died before his time. "Hmm..." John replied, "It's no wonder when you work with these types, early retirement takes on a whole other meaning," he said, changing the topic back to Christian.

"So, you're telling me that Christian can do all that stuff just like old Arnold?"

"Yes, and then some," Katheryn replied. "But please remember, you can't say a word of this to anyone. It's not only Christian I'm worried about... it's you, Debra and Amy."

"I understand and thank you, but there's no need for you to go worrying about us now. We can handle ourselves pretty well," John said with a reassuring smile. "Now I understand the suits." He paused reflecting, "I knew they had something to do with what happened to Amy."

"Oh my god, Amy – we've got to get her out of there," Debra Kendall said excitedly.

Katheryn calmed her, "Don't worry, I'll call Edward. He said he was going to take care of her."

"Why? What does that mean?" Debra questioned nervously. Katheryn dialed.

"Hi Jennifer, this is Katheryn Asher, is Edward there?"

There was a long pause, "Why no, didn't they tell you? Those people pulled him out of here minutes after you left."

"What do you mean, pulled him out of there?"

"They took him with them when they left with that other agent – you know, the one who shot the girl."

"What about Amy? Where is she? Did they take her?" Katheryn asked. Her concern was apparent to the Kendall's.

"I don't know how to tell you this, but her body is missing. Nobody knows where it is. All we know for sure is that it was gone before they left, and that bitchy one..."

"Kearns," Katheryn interrupted.

"Yep, that one; went ballistic when they couldn't find her body," the nurse whispered into the hand-cupped receiver of the phone.

"Thank you Jennifer, let me know if you hear anything..." Katheryn disconnected. She attempted to keep her composure as she explained what she had heard from the nurse, which brought Debra to tears once again.

"What did they do with my baby now?" she cried.

Mr. Kendall attempted to calm her, "Debra, you need to relax, Amy's fine. Edward has plenty of friends at the hospital. He probably moved her to keep her safe. At least we know those SOB's didn't get to her," he said in a calming voice, hiding his own concerns.

The hours passed slowly. The Kendalls stayed close to Katheryn, John taking on the protective role in Edward's absence. He made some calls to a few buddies who, although retired, refused to give up their military way of life. Two of them were full blown survivalists that had hardwired themselves into military society to keep abreast of everything. He requested they put an ear out for anything strange crawling on the military grapevine.

Katheryn contacted a number of doctors and friends of Edward's and hers, all with the same result. Not one of them knew he had been taken. She finished up with a call to Harold

"The Bull" Kellerman, a general that Edward had saved from multiple bullet wounds years earlier. He was unavailable, out of town for a conference. After leaving a non-specific message, she sat quietly with the Kendall's, thinking of what to do next. The minutes passed like hours.

A tear rolled down Katheryn's face, her inner strength spent, she confessed, "I don't know what to do anymore. Those bastards are hunting my son like a wild animal. They took my husband god knows where... and now Amy's missing. I can't find anyone that knows anything. I just don't know what to do," she cried.

Debra put her arm around her and gently grabbed her hand, "Don't worry, we'll know something soon. Just be patient, something has to happen."

"Can I get you something... coffee or a drink?" asked John sympathetically.

"No, no thank you, I'll be fine. It's just this is everything I never thought would happen," she said, wiping the tears from her face.

"I know, I know... nobody could have expected this," said John supportively.

Davenport, blocked by a wall of smoke and flames and unable to continue his pursuit by car, called for secondary air support to replace the downed chopper. The closest available chopper was a News 12 chopper and they were refueling and over ten minutes out. He stood in defeat yet again as he watched the blue Monte fade into the distance through the occasional break of thick black smoke. He wondered what they were up against with Christian and his new friend. There was no doubt in his mind that this kid had some very unusual talents; the most obvious one of them was leaving agency property in ruins.

He yanked the earpiece from his ear, tired of listening to Kearns' incessant berating of the team's failure to apprehend Christian and his accomplice quickly, and then he thought back to his original order to pick up this kid. "Why?" he thought, "He had done nothing wrong, he committed no crime, he was only enjoying the New Year with his family and friends. What was it about this particular kid that lit the fire under her butt? How did he even get on her radar?"

Davenport realized that no one was ever hurt, outside of Morano, but then again, he rationalized, Morano did pull the trigger on him and hit his girlfriend. He questioned not only why, but how Christian was able to heal Morano. "Why would he go to such lengths and risk his capture to help someone who had hurt him so deeply?"

Two things were still on his mind. "Why was he so reckless today? He could have killed plenty of people when he dropped that chopper from the sky, and why was Kearns waging a personal war against him?" He'd soon have his answers.

"Lock it down," he ordered the agents arriving on scene. The service road now partially cleared, he watched other agency cruisers race along the westbound service road to continue their pursuit with hopes of finding the blue Monte minus one rear bumper somewhere up the road. As they pushed their cruisers to speed they noticed something very unusual in the distance.

CB pushed the ailing car westbound as he and Christian shook off the jitters of almost having their scalps split open by the rotor blade that had passed between them moments earlier.

"We're going to have to lose this car," CB said loudly over the whistling noise from the cold wind blowing through the split roof.

"Yeah, I know," Christian said as he surveyed the area for any remaining pursuers. "It looks pretty clear; why don't you get off at the next exit. We can dump it over there somewhere." CB agreed and moved right.

BAM! The car took a hit causing it to swerve wildly. Christian turned quickly looking behind him.

"What the hell was that?" CB asked. "Sounds like she's starting to fall apart. I don't think we're going to make the exit..." CB said.

"That wasn't the car," Christian said, referring to the loud crunching sound. His senses began to heighten.

"Then what was it?" asked CB, his senses starting to heighten as well.

BAM! The car jolted violently "What the hell is that?" CB yelled as the roof started to collapse. "What's going on?" He struggled to maintain control of the car with one hand while pushing back on the roof with the other.

Christian looked at CB, seriously concerned, crouching lower and lower in his seat as the collapsing roof pressed in on them. "I have no idea, but whatever it is, it's going to crush us!" he yelled. Heavy braided steel cables were now visible as they bounced off the front and sides of the car.

"This is crazy!" CB shrieked. "Who the hell is this?"

"Hit the brakes and jump," Christian yelled over the sound of the tortured roof collapsing. CB slammed on the brakes. The tires locked, causing the car to skid wildly.

"The doors won't open... I can't get out!" CB yelled.

"Holy shit! What the hell is that?" yelled Christian as heavy steel claws clamped down on the Monte's doors, crushing them. The Sikorski was locked on and dragging the Monte down the road.

"We have to get out of here... I'll go out the back, you take the front," CB yelled, straining to squeeze his way between the bucket seats and onto the glass-filled back seat. Christian kicked out the remainder of windshield and started to work his way to the hood of the car.

The car swerved violently as the helicopter began to lift the unstable load, throwing Christian out onto the hood. Christian held on for dear life as the weight of the car shifted in between the massive steel claws.

Now dangling from the driver's side of the car, Christian struggled to maintain his grip. "CB...CB, where are you?" he yelled. There was no answer.

"Where the hell is this guy going?" Christian asked, looking down to find himself hanging two hundred feet above the roadway. His grip failing, Christian stretched to reach a loose steel cable hanging from the claw. "Two more inches... got it!" He started to pull himself up the greasy lifeline, the frayed wires slicing into his hands as he worked his way up the cable to climb back into the car.

"CB... CB... where are you?" he called out again. His call was unanswered. Craning his neck he searched for CB as he pulled himself up and climbed back into the empty car. His fear of what was happening had faded, replaced by mournful concern. He stared out the back window looking for signs of his friend below.

The flying wasp turned north toward the expressway as Christian's hopes faded.

Agency cruisers in pursuit had received reports of an early model blue Monte Carlo racing westbound just ahead of them. Davenport clicked in, "Can you see them?" he asked anxiously.

"Not yet, sir. I'm sure they are just ahead of us."

Davenport clicked in again, "The locals have blocked the road a couple of miles in front of you. I think their luck has just run out," he said confidently. Tension grew as the moments passed and the agents raced to close in behind the Monte.

"Sir, you're not going to believe this..." the agent clicked in apprehensively.

Davenport responded, "I'm not going to believe what?" he asked in a stern but curious voice. "Can you see them?"

"Yes, sir."

"Well, where are they?" he asked.

"They're headed north, sir."

"Are you in pursuit?" he asked.

"No sir, we are standing down."

"Standing down my ass, you stay with them," he ordered.

"We can't, sir."

"Why the hell not?" Davenport asked angrily.

"Because they are travelling north two hundred feet above us, sir."

"What the hell does that mean?"

"Just what I said, sir. They are headed north two hundred feet above us. Some strange looking helo dropped a claw on them and picked them up."

"That's the bastard we were trying to clear from the area... Can you see any markings?" asked Davenport.

"No sir... nothing."

With veins popping from his forehead, Davenport grabbed his binoculars and looked west. "Son of a bitch!" He slammed his fist on the car. "How the hell does he do it?" he groaned as he watched his prey fly away. "Follow him and keep me posted on their location."

"Yes, sir," the agent responded, heading north to follow.

"And contact ATC. I want to know where they're going," he barked.

"Where the hell is that other damn chopper? I need them here now... Got it?" he called out to the field office as he slammed the mic down angrily.

Kearns, listening to the action play out back at the command trailer, went ballistic. She blasted her team, trying to find out what happened and who was responsible. Davenport could hear her rantings from his earpiece dangling on his shoulder. He smirked.

"This kid's really starting to get under my skin," she mumbled to herself and stormed out of the command trailer. Her last order was "Get me the mother! I want to talk to her. Hold her on anything you want. Jaywalking for all I care. Just bring her to me," she demanded. "It's time for a little family reunion," she grinned devilishly, formulating her next steps.

– Five –
Twenty-one Hours

Christian sat quietly devastated over the loss of Amy and now his friend as he moved north two hundred feet above the ground. A world of questions raced through his mind; "Who is this? What do they want? Where are they taking me?" The questions kept coming, but he had no answers. His thoughts were with Amy and CB.

The only thing he could think to do was to connect with Akachi and Hwei Ru. Sensing urgency they opened themselves to him. Through their telepathic connection they could see all that was happening.

Hwei Ru told him not to worry, that all would reveal itself, and that he was more than capable of handling what was to come. She reminded him to think carefully and remember her words from when they first connected. Akachi vowed he would be there to help when he needed it, which took Christian by surprise. "What do you mean when I need it?" Christian said confused.

"I think you and CB have it covered for now," said Akachi.

"CB, what do you mean? He fell out of the car," Christian said, curious about Akachi's lack of concern.

"Look out the window," Akachi laughed.

Christian stuck his head out the window and looked down to see CB hanging from the axle looking up at him. He forced a smile as Christian helped him climb into the car in the cold February air.

"Jesus! I thought you were dead," Christian smiled, happy to see his friend.

"Well, we're not out of hot water yet. Why don't you pull me in first and then we can chat. It's a little cold out here," CB said, shivering.

Christian pulled him in. "It's not much better in here." They said farewell to their friends and disconnected, but not before Hwei Ru again reminded Christian of their private chat and told him to be strong.

"Remember the way…" she said, trying to guide Christian deeper into his memories.

Hwei Ru knew something more about Christian than she let on. There was something special about him… very special even among his kind, but she knew that he would have to find this out on his own. No one, not even Van Dunne, could guide him there. She also knew his life would depend upon learning this sooner rather than later.

Together again, Christian celebrated CB's survival. "Why didn't you just climb in?" he asked.

"I tried to, but my hands stiffened up quickly from the cold and I didn't want to risk losing my grip and falling." He shivered, rubbing his arms vigorously in an attempt to warm them.

"You could have called for me!" Christian said as if the thought had not crossed CB's mind.

"I did, but you can hardly hear me in here when I'm sitting next to you. I gave up after a minute of yelling for you and sensed you reach out to connect with Akachi and Hwei Ru, so I connected with them, too."

"Why didn't you just connect with me?" he asked.

"I did… You weren't answering."

"I was a little preoccupied…" Christian defended.

The pair planned what they were going to do when they touched down, if in fact, they did touch down. Minutes later the helicopter started to descend. They peered out of the collapsed windows as the flying wasp lined itself up with a tractor trailer moving at speed on the expressway. The turbulent air passing over the truck mixing with the rotor wash caused the car to pitch and sway as the pilot maneuvered closer to make his delivery.

"What the hell is he doing?" CB asked nervously, "Is he going to drop us on that trailer?" As the words passed his lips the flying wasp released its magnetic grip and dropped its prey. The seconds moved slowly as they dropped toward the trailer. Falling nose first afforded the edgy passengers a view of the quickly approaching container roof.

Bracing themselves for impact they watched as the car hit the roof and passed right through it. BAM! The car slammed onto the deck of the container. "Did you see that? How did that happen?" Christian groaned, banged up from the impact, "We passed right through it!" CB did not respond, he just observed quietly, a concerned look on his face.

The tired Monte, billowing smoke and steam, creaked as it settled on the deck of the container. The hiss of air racing from punctured tires echoed in the container as pools of antifreeze and oil poured from the exhausted V-8.

"Look at that!" Christian shouted, staring at the roof of the container. He studied the now transparent roof. It looked more like an electrical haze. A series of bright beams of light began passing from the front of the container to the back, each accompanied by a strange electrical hum as the roof appeared to solidify. The roof of the trailer, now fully formed, sealed them in the rolling casket as it travelled to destinations unknown.

"I've got a bad feeling about this," CB expressed his concern "It's an electrochemical barrier. Who in the world could possibly have this technology?" he wondered.

Christian's inquisitive side took the helm, at least for the moment, with his attention fixed on the unusual container roof. "That was amazing! The molecular density of the roof changed... It allowed us to pass right through, and then solidified. I've seen that somewhere before," he thought.

It struck them both at the same time. They knew where they had seen this before. They looked at each other and swallowed hard, "Do you remember?" CB asked.

"Yep..." The reply was short, but the facial expression told it all. "This can't be good."

Christian caught the scent of a familiar odor. "Hurry, cover your face," he yelled as the container began to fill with the sweet and sour smelling gas he had succumb to once before.

"What the hell is this?" CB asked, his words slurring quickly under the effects of the gas.

Christian's attempts to communicate with CB went unanswered as he too faded out.

The trailer traveled westbound, it's final destination a mid-island airport named for General MacArthur. The driver quickly pulled into a large hanger toward the end of the runway.

Ryan Jennings, the air traffic controller, was just coming back from a fact-finding mission. Noticing the unmarked trailer pulling into the hanger, he thought it peculiar and hurried around back to see what was happening.

"What the hell is this?" he questioned under his breath, capturing a glimpse of the unusual activity through a partially opened window. He watched as a strangely uniformed crew of six disembarked the back of a cargo plane waiting in the hanger to off-load the trailer container that had just arrived. Not so strange, but it was how they did it that shocked him. Two lines of three crew members apiece walked to each side of the trailer. One of the crew waved his hand, opening a panel on the side of the container. Jennings strained to see exactly what was happening, but his view was partially obscured by cartons next the window. What he witnessed next couldn't be explained. The container changed shape before his eyes. He rubbed his eyes in disbelief as the roof and sides of the container collapsed until it was two thirds of its original size. The corners rounded as it took on a shape more like that of an old silver airstream travel trailer.

Dumbfounded, he watched what was happening as the crew of six positioned around the trailer lifted the reshaped container and started to carry it into the cargo bay.

"Holy crap, they're not even touching it," he said before realizing he was no longer using his inner monologue. The crew's dark eyes turned in his direction as he ducked out of sight. Seconds later he stood up for another look only to find the container was already loaded in the back of the plane.

"That's impossible," he calculated. That couldn't have been more than five or ten seconds."

The flight crew hurried to secure the reshaped twenty-eight foot trailer to a trolley in the back of the plane and locked it down to the deck. The plane's cargo door closed quickly and the plane readied for departure.

Grabbing his phone he called the ATC. "It's Ryan, keep your eyes on this one leaving hanger C for me."

"Sorry, sir, no can do. The system's down. We are on visual only," the ATC reported.

"How can that be?" he asked.

"I don't know sir. It went down just after we cleared that heavy lifter in hanger C to land, the one you're talking about. Everything is blank," ATC replied.

"I'll be there in a minute, get it back online ASAP," Ryan urged as he watched the hanger doors close behind the plane.

The heavy lifter taxied out to the runway, received clearance for departure and throttled up. It rolled down the runway and lifted off sluggishly as the four blade props grabbed the air to climb and headed east out over the Atlantic before banking to a southerly course.

– Six –
The Early Years

Trapped and unconscious, Christian drifted off, entering a dream state that would lead him to relive a life he had long forgotten... his early years.

A blurry image came into focus. It was of a house that was very familiar to him. It was the same house Christian saw in his dreams at his parent's home over the holidays, but somehow it was more familiar this time. The details of the home were vivid. He could picture every aspect of the house, especially the layout of a young boy's room; the light blue paint and tan carpet, his toy box in the corner holding his army soldiers, toy planes, and a large collection of model spaceships and Star Wars™ type figures. There were coloring books on the bottom of his night stand and a laptop on his desk, but not just any laptop, a top of the line Alienware® laptop. "Why would such a young boy have the need for such a powerful laptop?" he questioned.

The boy's pajamas were folded neatly over the back of a chair. Sitting on his bed was a large stuffed bear missing one eye he called "Shizid." His baseball cap was hanging from a low hook on the back of the door, and a baseball signed by Derek Jeter perched atop his dresser next to a small aquarium holding two seahorses whom he referred to as his "Atlantians." His box of private possessions hidden in his "secret spot" under his bed held small amounts of money from all over the world that his uncle had given him from his travels. His baseball cards, football cards, Star Wars cards and the like were all neatly assorted and arranged in the box, along with his secret copy of a spaceman comic book that he remembered having to sneak into the house because his mom felt they influenced his habit of telling wild stories.

Entering the short hallway he could see the bowling trophies above the fireplace. The tallest was for a perfect game played some years earlier by the boy's father, his claim to fame.

As he moved to the living room he could see the grandfather clock with a crack across the bottom of the glass door from when the boy's mother had accidently struck it with the vacuum cleaner. The pillows on the couch, once brightly colored, were now faded from the sun, one of which covered an old stain. And of course, the pictures on the wall were filled with people that seemed all too familiar.

"What is this, dream or reality?" Everything was so clear, except for the dark haired little boy. "Who were these people and who was this little boy? Why can't I see his face?" he wondered. The dream faded into a blur and what was hours seemed to pass in only moments as he moved deeper into his memories. His mind flashed to another more unsettling scene at the young boy's home.

Upon entering the house the boy's unnerved mother stormed up to her husband without a greeting and blurted, "He's doing it again!"

"Doing what again?" he asked.

"It's starting again, just like last time, and the time before, and the time before that," said the mother angrily.

The man, now appearing a bit unsettled himself, glared at his son standing quietly in the living room briefly before attempting to calm the woman down.

"OK, tell me what happened," the man said, glaring again at the boy.

The disturbed women appeared as if she would pull the hair from her head as she paced back and forth between the small living room and dining room. "Do you know what it's like to hear him say, 'Mommy, this is where I died... Remember?'" She continued her ranting. "Then he tells me this crazy story about how he was helping his father change a tire by the bridge when a car hit him and sent him flying over the bridge and onto the rocks, and then he says it again, 'That's where I died... Remember?' I can't take this anymore! He needs to see someone."

"But I did die," the dark haired little boy claimed sadly.

The boy's father yelled loudly at his son. "You know how this makes us feel, hearing these crazy stories from you! We can't go through this again. I just can't!" he exclaimed. "More doctors, more questions from the school and those psychiatrists. Screw that, I can't do it!"

The woman tried reassuring herself that it was just a story and it might not be the same as stories he told before, even if he did tell them with remarkable accuracy. She struggled to find another answer to how the boy could have come up with a story like this. After all, he's only five and this was far different from the stories he told in the past.

"You haven't been watching scary movies with him have you?" she asked.

"Of course not," the husband replied, coming up with a quick solution to show the boy he was wrong.

"Look, let's settle this once and for all. What's the name of that bridge?" he asked.

"Dalton," she replied.

"OK, let's check it out." The man walked over to his desk, pulled the chair out aggressively, then sat down and began typing.

Christian could see everything as if it were him typing. *Boy dies on Dalton Bridge*, enter. The husband looked up at his wife and before he could say a word he saw the horror in her face. Spinning back to view the computer screen he was staring at the title of an article, *Little boy killed last night on Dalton Bridge*. His face paled as he turned and walked away without a word.

The woman moved closer and began to read the description of the incident which had occurred some five years earlier and seemed an exact match to the little boy's story. Numerous accounts of the incident popped up on the screen. *Boy Dies on Dalton Bridge, Child Struck and Killed, Tragedy on the Dalton Bridge, Bridge of Death Claims Another Victim*.

The first of the stories read, "*A family outing turned tragic last night when a couple, along with their five year old son, were stranded on the roadside at the entrance to Dalton Bridge. After getting a flat tire, the father pulled off the roadway to make his repair. According to witnesses, the boy was standing by the passenger rear of the car next to his father, helping him change the tire when a speeding vehicle skidded on the rain soaked roadway, colliding with the disabled vehicle. The little boy (name withheld at the family's request) was struck and thrown some twenty feet over the guardrail and plummeted to his death fifty feet below on the rocky shoreline. The five year old was pronounced dead at the scene. His father was hospitalized with a concussion and broken arm. The mother was inconsolable and unavailable for comment.*"

"*The driver of the speeding car was arrested for driving while intoxicated and possession of illegal substances. Details on page...*"

As the woman read the story in a quivering voice, Christian relived the tragic events of that night. He could see through the little boy's eyes as if it were him on the bridge as the speeding car approached, skidded and struck him and his dad. He could sense the impact and feel his limp body flying through the air and dropping to the jagged rocks beneath the bridge. As he lay there motionless, Christian felt the boy's light slowly fade. Taking his last breath, Christian sensed the life force raising from the boys shattered body.

Rising upward he could see his limp, lifeless body lying on the rocks beneath him, trickles of blood flowing from his ears, nose and mouth, his crystal blue eyes eerily open and staring into the cloudy night sky. He could see the boy's hysterical mother and injured father frantically trying to reach their son's lifeless corpse below with the help of other motorists who had stopped immediately to help the distraught couple. He felt a sense of peace, warmth and calm as he lifted further away. Suddenly there was a bright flash. He could feel the boy and himself being pulled toward a brightly lit swirling vortex. Christian started to feel himself being sucked into the vortex.

His life force rapidly accelerated through the brightly lit tunnel with blinding multi-colored lights flashing by like the white lines on a highway. Silvery blues and whites, light green, pinks and oranges all merged together as he continued to accelerate through the kaleidoscopic vortex at a nauseating velocity. Then as quickly as it began, there was a tremendous flash of bright white light. It was quiet, peaceful and warm. The light slowly faded, yielding to darkness and calm.

It seemed as if only moments had passed before he heard, "Push... Push... you're doing great... one last P-U-U-U-U-SH," and then he felt frightened, cold and wet. Struggling to open his eyes, a blurry world slowly came into focus.

It was a lady with brown hair darkened from perspiration, a large vein across her forehead, watery, pink-shaded eyes with a bright smile and tears of joy; the little boy's mother coddled her newborn. Looking down at him and then to her husband she said, "Let's call him Christian."

Christian felt sickened at the sound of his own name as he began to remember what he had blocked out many years earlier. The events of his early years that he so tried to suppress were now a nightmare playing out over and over in his mind as he lay unconscious. He was the little boy…

He faded in and out of his dream state under the effects of the gas.

He continued to remember the reality of early childhood. It was no longer a dream. Now it was a bad memory buried long ago that came back to haunt him.

After an hour with a scotch bottle his father had calmed down enough to return. He called Christian back to the living room. Christian watched himself as a young boy walk from his childhood bedroom into a barrage of questions more suited to an adult's ear. He simply responded, "I did die, I did," and ran into the next room. Hearing those words again, "I did die," enraged the upset woman. She glared at her husband, waiting for him to present a solution to this madness.

"OK, OK, I understand you're upset but maybe there's some other explanation this time…" the man addressed his wife, doubting his own statement as the words left his mouth after having experienced this all too many times over the past few years. He turned to look at his son and he was gone. He called out to him, "Christian Bradley, you get over here right now!" he demanded. Christian walked back into the room with a cold, sad look on his face. He was both annoyed and upset that his parents would not believe him.

His mother lost it, "You see, I can't put up with this anymore." The father agreed. He ordered the young boy to go to his room. As the boy reached his room his father stormed in and grabbed his laptop. "No more computer for you. Maybe if you don't have this thing in your room, you won't be able to come up with these crazy stories. Now stay here and think about how you upset your mother, and don't come out until I tell you to," he ordered angrily.

The very next day they reluctantly accompanied Christian to school and met with the school psychiatrist. They explained the events of the day before, which was at the beginning of their long list of concerns. The doctor agreed with them, Christian's claim to be the boy on the bridge was highly unlikely and he questioned the young boy.

"Now Christian, I think we both know that it's not possible that you were the boy who was hurt on the bridge, now don't we?" he asked.

Christian looked up at him with eerie confidence and answered, "Not hurt, killed."

The newly appointed school psychiatrist argued his point to the deaf ears of a first grader. Being unfamiliar with the history he looked at the parents and questioned, "Is this the only incident or have there been others?" The parents looked at each other, distressed, and started to rattle off a number of the many events that had transpired up to this point.

The father started, "When he was two I was trying to set up a new entertainment system. I had worked on it for hours and was very frustrated when he walked up to me and smiled."

"He connected every wire and had programmed the entire entertainment system within ten minutes. I was working on it for over two hours," he said, almost complaining of his shortcomings.

"The mother chimed in, "I was shopping with him in the mall and he walked up to a complete stranger and said, 'Hi Billy, how's it going?'

"Well maybe he knew him from school?" the doctor suggested.

"No, he didn't. That boy didn't even go to his school, he went to school in Smithfield two towns over.

"Well that doesn't sound so bad, kids often meet each other during events and at playgroups," the doctor added.

"The boy was six years older than him and he knew everything about him; how old he was, his birthday, where he lived, who his friends were, what school he went to, and his parents' names as well. Christ, he even asked about his golden retriever, 'Dodger", who they named after the "Artful Dodger," you know, the thief from "Oliver Twist", because he was always steeling food from the counter."

"It scared the crap out of me, but the little boy freaked when Christian said he was his old friend, Tommy. This upset the boy to no end. He just looked at him horrified and ran off without another word."

The doctor listened intently over the next hour as the parents rattled off a series of events that had occurred involving Christian's unique talents. He released the parents and pondered the stories he heard while quietly walking Christian back to his classroom in order to explain why the boy was so late to class that morning.

As they approached the classroom they could hear the class shouting answers to questions asked by the teacher. "Ooh, it sounds like math class." He smiled at Christian who returned the gesture. The teacher had seconds earlier asked another question when he opened the door. The students had just started to shout their answers.

The classroom grew eerily quiet when Christian entered the room followed by the doctor. "Look whose back," the teacher smiled uncomfortably, "OK everyone, let's welcome Christian back..." The meekest of greetings was offered up by the class.

Christian was awakened by a loud screeching sound reso-
nating inside the trailer as it began to slide and vibrate. The
temporary saving grace pulled him from his memory driven
nightmare and into a state of semi-consciousness.

When the school psychologist returned to his office that day
he dug to the bottom of his file drawer and pulled out a second
file containing more reports referencing Christian's behavior.
The file was rather large for such a young student. As he read
through the reports he saw complaint after complaint from
teachers that Christian had "corrected" over the course of his
short matriculation at the school.

Normally teachers welcome questions and even the occasional challenge from their students. It helps to develop a
child's learning and communication skills as well as teaching
them not to take all they hear and see at face value; however,
some teachers have a tendency to get insulted when they are
challenged by a student in front of the class, especially one so
young and headstrong. In their eyes it takes away their position
of authority, and the fact that Christian was so persistent made
matters worse. Adding insult to injury, in most all cases he was
actually correct and proved it to them.

The list was long and included a science teacher who accidently
mixed the wrong chemicals during a demonstration. He intended
to show a simple exothermic reaction to the class. This usually
got the class excited when they saw the nontoxic steamy
foam rise up out of the flask and pour out onto the lab table.
What he hadn't counted on was being interrupted by another
student before adding the final components that would cause
the reaction.

After answering the student's question he rushed to complete
the demonstration and inadvertently grabbed the wrong flask,

grabbing one that contained an acidic mixture and poured it in with the existing components at the same time as he added the potassium iodide. Once added, it generated a progressive reaction that was sure to explode violently. Christian, seeing the teacher's mistake, ran up to the table, grabbed the smoldering flask from the startled teacher and tossed it out the window before the teacher even realized what he had done. The flask exploded only seconds after being dropped from the window and sprayed an area over twenty feet in diameter with glass and a hot acid-based liquid that scored the side of the building and damaged the paint on a half dozen cars parked in the teacher's lot below.

The principal's report included both sides of the story. The teacher admitted that he was embarrassed by the situation and more so when Christian explained in detail what he did wrong in front of the class, the reason he was sent to the principal's office. Christian was much more thorough in his description of the event. He explained how the teacher was distracted and then discussed each component that was mixed and why it resulted in an explosion. A notation on the bottom of the report stated, when asked how he knew it was going to explode, Christian replied, "I've seen it happen before," followed by three question marks.

Next was a long list of complaints, mostly from his two history teachers, citing multiple cases where he insisted the books they were using to educate the class were incorrect. In one of the most infamous cases his teacher was referencing a more advanced history text to show the class differences in technology across the ages. During the lesson he mentioned that the Sumerians and Minoans were the oldest civilizations to have used simple technology like water pumps, basic plumbing and simple devices used as calendars to mark the time of year. Christian argued the timeline of the oldest known civilizations with the teacher, stating that the Sumerians and Minoans were far from being the oldest civilizations to have advanced technology and that they possessed much more advanced technology than was referenced in the text.

His point fell on deaf ears because there was no way to prove his statements to them at the time. Christian knew well that the truth of his statements could only have been proven with a field trip to the region where the yet undiscovered archeological sites lay in wait to be discovered. The locations were some five thousand miles away, located near Egypt and throughout northern Africa, and would have to wait to be discovered to prove him right.

Although prepared to continue his debate and offer up the names and locations of many ancient cities currently unknown to history and all lying beneath the sands of time, he never had the chance. After being reprimanded by the teacher he was escorted from the room to the sound of laughing classmates, and made to wait in the principal's office until the lesson was over.

In another case his correction of the teacher and the text book she was referencing from was proven shortly afterward with the discovery of an archeological find during a 2000-2001 underwater excavation near the site of Alexandria in the Mediterranean Sea by an underwater archeologist named Franck Goddio.

This particular dispute had to do with a city called Heracleion, the Greek name for the "mythical" city the teacher was discussing in class that very first day of school. It was also called Thonis, which was the Egyptian name for it.

During the class, the teacher began to educate her young students on terms they would be hearing during the school year. As she read from the latest edition text books issued by the Department of Education for her lessons during the school year, she began to discuss ancient cities with the class, starting with the definition of ancient.

When she reached the topic of mythical cities she started talking about the city of Heracleion or Thonis. She explained, "This city is considered to be a myth or mythical city." She defined myth and mythical for her young students and continued to explain why. "It is considered to be a mythical city because, aside from the occasional mention in ancient texts," she defined occasional and texts, and continued to state, "there was no evidence to suggest this city had actually existed."

Christian interrupted stating, "It isn't a myth, and the city actually existed. It was the main port of entry to Egypt for Greek shipping until it was taken by the sea about 1500 years ago." The teacher, baffled by his claim, argued the point with him stating there was no evidence to support that this city ever existed, but Christian insisted and continued to debate with her.

He described the city in detail; the walls of carved stone with brick and stone laid streets, and the combination of art-work of both Egyptian and Greek influence, depending on what sector of the city you were referring to. He described the enormous statues chiseled from stone and marble by master artisans that adorned the entrance to the port city, along with elaborate murals and mosaic wall and floor art, and then he mentioned Helen of Troy's visit to a magnificent temple built in the Southern central part of the city where she paid homage to the Gods, the temple of Amun, or Herakles as he was called by the Greeks.

The teacher's patience had reached its end just as he began to describe the violent events that had, over time, taken the mythical city to its now shallow resting place in the Mediterranean, just a few short miles from today's coastline. The teacher ended the conversation abruptly by sending Christian to the principal's office.

The school psychologist continued to read the reports with increasing interest. He read through the school principal's notes next, at least the ones associated with Christian's repeated visits to her office. Her notes read more like a diary. She always kept them for each eventful school day when any student was sent to her office, which pretty much meant she kept a daily log.

That day's entry read, "Although I was less than thrilled to have my first visitor of the year so early on the first day of school, I found that I would see things in a different light after the curious but enlightening conversation I had with young Mr. Williamson. He is a remarkably gifted boy with either the greatest of imaginations or insight far beyond our average students."

"I am almost certain that with the way my day had started, I looked at him with less than sympathetic eyes when I asked him, 'Can you tell me why you are here already Mr. Williamson?'"

"I remember young Christian smiled meekly and explained the story to me in detail. I was amazed with his knowledge of ancient history and impressed with the words he used to describe his position in defending his statements to his teacher, Ms. Thermopolas."

The doctor continued to read Ms. Thermopolas' thorough accounts of incidents involving Christian. While reading the report from the first day of school he found something most unusual, something he had missed earlier. She claimed that Christian recited his side of the story in perfect Greek.

She noted, "Christian was becoming increasingly insistent with his claims, which admittedly was a frustrating way to begin the first day of the school year. I felt that the time he had used debating his point was taking far too long and in the interest of the other students I elected to dismiss him from the morning lesson and have him wait in the principal's office. It was only after seeing the confused look of the other students that I realized that Christian was arguing his point in Greek the entire time. I must admit I was taken aback by this as he was not speaking as a child would speak; he spoke at an advanced level, grammatically and with the clarity and enunciation of a scholar using perfect tone, pitch and inflection."

The doctor, knowing Ms. Thermopolas long enough, knew that she grew up with old world parents and only spoke the Greek language at home. It wasn't a far cry to say she understood everything he said and there was no reason to doubt her or think she may be mistaken as to the level of language Christian used to debate the matter. She graduated "Suma Cum Laude," with highest honors, held an exemplary record and was, to say the least, over qualified for most positions in the education department.

He read on, learning that Ms. Thermopolas was more than a little unnerved with this extraordinary display of knowledge, she was also intrigued by him, and decided to investigate Christian's abilities further by calling his parents in for a conference later that day at school.

Her report indicated the Williamson's arrived as scheduled at her office at the end of the school day. They appeared noticeably agitated and acknowledged Christian's presence with a less than affectionate glance. The discussion of the day's events served only to anger the parents who provided curt answers to any to questions posed during the hour long meeting.

She requested that Christian repeat what he said in class and he did, but not in fluent Greek as he did in class. Her continued attempts to extract the information from Christian in Greek served only to agitate Christian's parents who glanced at him with trepidation off and on throughout the interview. Tired of the constant questioning and curiosity by everyone, from their friends and neighbors to the mailman and just about every school official, nurse and psychiatrist that worked in the school district, they ended the meeting abruptly. Grabbing Christian by the arm they led him out of the office, making no excuses.

He read on. The very next day in class she often turned her gaze to him, trying to figure out why he didn't answer her questions the way he did the day before in class. It was eating away at her until she released the class from the days' lesson and pulled young Christian to the side and asked him, "γιατί δεν θα μου απαντήσετε στα ελληνικά χθες;" or "Why didn't you answer me in Greek yesterday?"

Christian smiled, "Because my mother and father get very upset when I speak in languages that they do not understand." Once again, in flawless Greek.

Astonished by his statement she asked, "Can you speak other languages?"

Christian smiled at her. "Yes," he said with an eerie confidence while fiddling with his school books.

"How many languages can you speak?" she inquired.

His answer would shock her and test her abilities to comprehend the depth of his knowledge. "I don't really know. I guess all of them and some others too."

Standing in awe of his claim, she elected to secretly put him to the test. She arranged to meet with him briefly every day the following week for a talk with her and the head of the language department who had studied linguistics for years. Each day that following week the linguist presented Christian with a series of questions in different languages; written, spoken, ancient and new. The linguist, having minored in ancient languages in college, asked his final question in the ancient language of Sanskrit, a virtually dead language established thousands of years ago that, despite limited usage for religious proceedings, has all but ceased to be used.

Christian smiled knowingly and replied, "I don't know how I can speak these languages," in Sanskrit.

The linguist sat stunned with mouth open, floored by his response, that Christian had responded to all questions correctly, and all in the languages in which the questions originated.

Mrs. Thermopolis' final entries following the sessions with the linguist read, "Upon advising him that our intent was to advance him to higher learning facilities so he could share his gift with the world he replied, "No, thank you. It would upset my parents."

The last entry was most curious, "Immediately following the final session we hurried back to watch the videos we recorded throughout the week. Our excitement was short lived, however, as there was nothing but static. What was most peculiar was the equipment recorded everything prior to our sessions and after, nothing in between."

This was enough for the doctor to act. With his interest peaked, he elected to call a friend of his in to discuss Christian. This was his area of specialty. He travelled the world to talk with children with similarly unique talents. His voicemail picked up. "Hi, Dr. Stedwell, it's Brian Thatcher. I have someone that might interest you. He's pretty special... give me a call."

Her curiosity peaked, Ms. Thermopolis studied Christian's activities closely for the remainder of the school year, testing him occasionally on various topics. She reviewed her personal file on him regularly as she updated her notes, but there was one thing she had overlooked repeatedly while reviewing the file, one small part of the statement made by the young boy the day after she first met with him and his parents. A key part of his statement that, later on in life, she would come to realize just how important to her work he was. That statement was, "And some others too."

She conversed daily with other teachers and learned what new things he did or said in their classrooms. She documented each occurrence in which he displayed his remarkable talents and was unrelenting with her investigation of this curious little boy. Additionally, she acted as the gateway to the boy and spoke on a regular basis with Dr. Thatcher's colleague, Dr. Stedwell. He had introduced them early in the year because he knew that Ms. Thermopolas' notes would be helpful to his friend. He also knew that they shared one trait in particular aside from their mutual interest in Christian; they were both meticulously thorough and well documented.

During the school year Christian often caught her gaze and would ask her what she wanted to know, which became quite unsettling to her. "How did he know I was watching?" she would think to herself. "Is it possible... could it be that he can actually read my thoughts?"

She realized the power of observation during this time. It brings focus to a task and lines up the pieces of information so the one observing can make discoveries that would pass by the nonobservant. Her conclusion, "There is something incredibly different, even special about this child, and whatever it is, I have to know what it's all about."

That summer break, Thermopolas, at the urging of Dr. Stedwell, decided to change her career path. She enrolled in Harvard University and earned her psychiatric degree within two years and then entered a special services branch of the U.S. Government. During her first year in service she married a Special Forces commander named Jimmy Kearns. Their relationship ended tragically when his truck was reportedly hit by an RPG only months after their marriage.

Christian and CB moved in and out of consciousness during the first part of their trip in the container, each left to his own memories. For Christian this was a time of discovery as he continued to relive the nightmare that he had suppressed years earlier.

Fading back into his dream-state he found himself hiding, frightened, behind his bedroom door. His father was drunk and yelling loudly. He felt himself flinch each time his father smashed another object in the house. His mother's attempts to calm him fell short. He threw her violently against the wall and started to strike the wall next to her in his rage.

He remembered running to her side after one of his father's vicious blows connected and knocked her to the floor. He tried desperately to pull her up, wanting to bring her to his room to hide from his father's drunken rage. She looked at him, not with sympathy for the event he was forced to witness, but with a glare of revulsion. She pulled herself up from the floor and pushed him back to his room. The boy turned and watched through the partially open doorway just as his father threw a heavy vase, smashing it against the wall. The glass fractured and sprayed the woman, cutting her face and arms.

Her hands, trembling and bloodied, again pushed the boy into his room and pulled the door shut. The frightened little boy sat helplessly on his bed, flinching with each strike of another object crashing against the wall during his father's increasingly violent tirade. The minutes passed as if they would never end. Then, silence. For a fleeting moment he heard nothing. B-A-N-G! The unmistakable sound of a gunshot rang throughout the house. The silence returned.

The boy exited his room and fearfully walked into the living room. The smell of burnt gunpowder filled his nostrils. His mother was sitting in the corner, whimpering uncontrollably. Her eyes were puffy and red from crying. She had cuts on her arms, legs and face from pieces of shattered glass and porcelain figurines her husband had thrown at her. She was splattered with blood and had pieces of flesh hanging from her blood-soaked blouse and hair. On the wall where she was standing only seconds before he pulled the trigger was the splatter of blood, eerily making a silhouette of her body, a reminder of the horror of the day that would remain uncleansed.

"Where are we?" CB slurred after a sudden jolt of the container brought the passengers to semi-consciousness.

"I think we're on the docks somewhere," Christian struggled to answer, the smell of stale water, salty air and the horn blasts of ships navigating the waters clueing them in.

"Where are they taking us now?" Christian wondered in the fleeting moments of clarity.

The container was loaded onto the top of a large, fully-loaded freighter, the nine hundred foot Olympus as another burst of paralyzing gas was released. Christian struggled to stay alert, but the effects of the gas were too strong. Shortly after pushing off from the dock, the combination of the gas and the gentle rocking motion of the Olympus underway pushed them back into their chemically induced slumber.

Christian re-entered his dream state, finding himself sitting in the back yard of the house he used to call home.

"Hi, Christian, is everything OK?" a neighbor inquired. He looked at his concerned neighbor and shrugged his shoulders with the look associated with uncertainty.

"It's awfully late, does your mom know you're out here?"

"Yes," he said nodding affirmatively. "The doors are locked."

"I'll be right over," the neighbor said, hurrying into his house to get his wife.

Minutes later the kind woman found Christian cold to the touch and wrapped him in her coat. She rubbed him vigorously to take the chill from his bones while her husband tried to gain entry to the house.

The police arrived moments later and broke in. Everyone had the same fear for what may have happened, especially with the memory of her husband's suicide still fresh in their minds. The police searched the home and found the woman hiding in a cabinet in the basement. One police officer shined a light on her, "I found her… in the basement. Better call an ambulance," he called out over his radio.

A half dozen officers rushed to the basement. When they arrived they were hit with the smell of death. "My god!" one officer said, "How long has she been dead?"

"She's not, but it sure looks like hell came to visit," his sergeant replied.

It was a horrific site. She was emaciated, unkempt and pale. Her face was sallow. She appeared not to have bathed or eaten in days or maybe weeks as she shivered, curled up in her hiding place.

When the police officers offered their hands to pull her up and remove her from the cabinet she shrieked, "He's not human, he's not human! Leave me alone, he's the devil! Leave me alone."

EMS arrived on scene, and with the aid of the police psychiatrist they escorted her to a waiting ambulance. When she saw her son standing with the neighbors she cried out, "Keep him away from me, keep him away."

He watched as his mother was taken by ambulance to the hospital, her ranting and raving forcing the psychiatrist to dose her with sedatives to protect her from injuring herself during the ride.

Christian stared with sad eyes as the ambulance drove off. The officer leaned forward and asked, "Are you OK buddy? How'd you like to take a ride in my police car? We can even use the lights," he said, pointing to the top of his police cruiser. Christian nodded his head affirmatively, climbed in the backseat and put his seatbelt on.

At the hospital, after receiving a clean bill of health, he softly asked the doctor, "Am I ever going to see my mom again?"

The doctor looked at him empathetically and said, "Maybe someday when she is all better. How would you like to pick out a toy to play with?" The young boy smiled as the doctor led him to a chest of old toys. He picked out a toy soldier, a GI Joe® that had only one hand and was missing its left eye, then climbed onto a chair in the waiting room.

As the boy played with his toy, a young woman covered in blood arrived in the ER. She was fighting the doctors and calling out the same words over and over. "Onde está meu bebê, onde está meu bebê?" The young boy couldn't help but notice that no one understood her request or that she was speaking Portuguese, so he hopped off his chair, put down his GI Joe and walked over to the team of doctors trying to stabilize the accident victim. After being shooed away twice he simply said, "All she wants to know is where her baby is," and turned and walked back to his seat.

The doctor, shocked that he understood the woman, approached him and politely requested his assistance in translating. He walked toward the distraught woman and smiled; his look calmed her almost instantly.

"Seu bebê está seguro com a família. Ela está ileso." He spoke softly telling her, "Your baby is safe with family and she is uninjured."

She placed her bloody hands on his face and kissed him gently on the forehead saying, "Obrigado, Obrigado meu anjo" – "Thank you, thank you my angel!"

Taking one of her hands, he leaned into her and whispered, "É OK para deixar ir. Sua bela do outro lado," – "It's OK to let go. It's beautiful on the other side..." and nodded his head with his boyish smile. The woman smiled calmly, a tear rolled down her cheek and she let go, her hand falling limp in his.

The doctors and nurses were amazed at what they had just witnessed. Staring at the boy they tried to grasp how such a young boy could have such a profound affect and connection with a woman he had never met before. His mere presence and a few spoken words calmed her instantaneously. The doctor especially admired the empathy he had for a woman he didn't even know, not to mention the courage he showed walking up to her when she was covered in blood and ranting like a wild woman. He took the boy by the hand and proceeded to clean him up. Bringing him back to his office, the boy fell fast asleep on the couch.

The doctor covered the young boy as he lay sleeping on the couch in his office. Sitting quietly at his desk he reviewed the mother's chart, taking special interest in the psych evaluation. The psychiatrist diagnosed a traumatic emotional psychosis as a result of the recent suicide of her husband. Basically he felt she had lost touch with reality as a result of this event. His notes described the depth of her psychosis by documenting the description of events that she vehemently insisted had occurred.

"Mrs. Williamson continued to rant that her son was the devil and/or a demon of some kind. She insisted he wasn't human, and produced a delusional account of events which she claimed had occurred shortly after the father's suicide. She states she was awakened by a strange buzzing sound and a bright light flashing in her son's room late one night. Upon opening the door she saw a bolt of lightning passing through him, raising him off the ground. She states she grabbed his arm, pulled him away from the bolt and dragged him out of the room. She continued with her account of events by stating a few days later she walked in on him staring into the bathroom mirror. When she looked at his reflection, it wasn't him; it was the reflection of some demonic creature, not her son's reflection. The psychiatrist's notes continued documenting her delusions. Mrs. Williamson continued stating that during the following nights she was awakened on multiple occasions by strange sounds coming from his room and when she went to investigate, she found her son sitting up in bed making strange noises like he was talking to someone, and that's when she claimed he turned his head and it wasn't her son, it was a demon from hell with dark eyes and a grey complexion. Mrs. Williamson broke down uncontrollably at this point and was sedated for her own safety.

The doctor glanced at the boy sleeping peacefully on his couch, knowing well he was now alone in the world. He made his decision...

Hours had passed before a loud screeching noise startled both of the container's passengers, waking them. The container was moving, but not smoothly. It felt as if something was nudging it along one push at a time. The screeching noise was so intense it hurt their ears, but that was the least of their problems. Semi-conscious and still unable to move without the greatest of effort, they felt the container sliding further and further.

"What the hell is going on now?" Christian wondered. The container tilted to one side and started to slide faster. It fell, flipping and twisting as it bounced off the back of the freighter and crashed into the dark waters below, the impact tossing the helpless passengers around the inside of the car.

Christian, panicking and unable to speak, attempted to connect with CB, "What the hell is going on?" The connection was weak and his communication fuzzy but understandable.

"I don't know. It feels like we're floating," CB said, straining to keep his telepathic connection open as the container rocked back and forth.

"I think so too. Are these things waterproof?" Christian asked nervously as the sound of water sloshing against the tin walls resonated loudly within.

"I hope so," CB replied, struggling.

"Oh crap! We're in big trouble!" Christian said, alarmed. "Look up!"

"I can't... what's happening?" Christian struggled to concentrate hard enough to share in real time what he was seeing. CB could now see through Christian's eyes as the water began to slosh over part of the container's semitransparent roof. "Oh shit, we're sinking," CB panicked.

"Maybe not," Christian said, keeping positive. "Maybe we're just floating like this because the car isn't centered in the trailer."

Wishful thinking. No sooner did he say that when they both felt the icy cold sea water wicking through the back of their seat, sending chills to their bones. The pair began to panic. Without being able to move and heighten their senses, they knew what fate lie before them. Quietly they pondered the inevitable as the pressure inside the container increased from the water forcing its way in.

CB sent out an alert to Hwei Ru, Akachi and all other fraternity members that had been awakened. "Christian and I captured by unknowns with advanced technology. Immobilized by gas. Trapped in sinking container in unknown body of water. Until we meet again... be careful my friends."

He didn't know if he reached anyone, his connection was weak, but his intent was honorable and it was well worth the try. That's what the fraternity is about, watching each other's backs, and warning them all that someone with resources and knowledge of them was around might save the lives of his friends.

The choppy waters continued to slap against the outside of the container. Still immobile, they watched nervously as the water crept over the top of their soon-to-be tomb.

– Seven –
Bag-em and Tag-em

Katheryn had answered most all of the Kendall's questions by the time they reached her home. An agency vehicle sitting across the street was an unnerving reminder of all that had happened earlier that day. Katheryn and the Kendall's managed to occupy their time reminiscing about what it was like raising their children. Long pauses in between their tales were filled with silence and the anxiety the events of the day had brought.

"Why hasn't Edward called? Doesn't he get a call or something?" Katheryn thought as she shared tales of Christian's escapades as a child and his uncanny ability to fix and create just about anything. Of course she omitted most all of his recently developed abilities, including the details of New Year's Eve, feeling that when it comes to this, the less the Kendall's know the better. But she did provide them with enough additional information to understand why the agency had such interest in him.

During their discussion John Kendall's cell phone rang. As soon as he answered it his eyes welled up and a smile covered his face. The ladies watched, wondering what could possibly make him smile with such grandness as he answered question after question with short responses, "Yes... OK... I will... OK... I'm glad you're..." As he was about to say goodbye to the caller the front door burst open with a loud crash; it was the agency. They stormed into the Asher home as if they were raiding a terrorist cell.

Another team entered from the rear, shattering the glass doors behind them and sending splintered wood and shattered glass flying through the once peaceful home as they surrounded the traumatized trio with guns drawn. One agent grabbed the phone out of John Kendall's hand. "Who is this?" he demanded abruptly. The phone fell silent. He looked at the call log intending to retrieve the caller's number but all it showed was 'private' caller.

"Hey, what the hell are you doing? That's my phone!" John said angrily as he reached to grab his phone.

The agent pushed him back. "Not anymore," he said callously as he put the phone in his pocket to bring back to command. Katheryn thought quickly. Her phone in hand, she pressed a couple of buttons and slid her phone under some papers.

"What's going on here?" John demanded to know, stepping up to the agent. He received no response. Two agents restrained him from behind.

"What do you want now? Haven't you bastards done enough to us?" Katheryn barked angrily. Her questions too, went unanswered. Seconds later a silhouette appeared in the doorway.

"You bitch! Where's my husband?" Katheryn cursed.

"It's nice to meet you as well. Mrs. Asher, I presume. Ah, and you must be the Kendall's. Search it, search it all," she ordered, strolling almost casually into the kitchen.

The agents ransacked the house again. "What are you looking for?" Kathryn demanded to know. Kearns sighed dramatically. "I think you know," she said.

"Mrs. Asher, we have a big problem. You and your husband, Edward isn't it, have been less than truthful with me about your son. You've interfered with a federal investigation and you've abducted a key witness, and quite frankly, I'm tired of it."

"Key witness, what the hell are you talking about. We didn't abduct anyone!" said Katheryn angrily.

"If you didn't abduct her, then where is she?" asked Kearns coldly.

"Where is who?" demanded Katheryn.

"Why Amy, of course... she's missing you know." She turned to the Kendall's to continue, "Did you help move her body or was it just the Asher's? It's not like she got up and walked out," she smiled, baiting them. She turned back to face Katheryn, "What's it going to take to get some answers out of you? Maybe..." she paused, "Maybe I'll let you see your husband before I lock him away."

Katheryn lunged at Kearns but was restrained by an agent. Kearns stood boldly.

"Now hold on a second lady. I don't know just who in the hell you think you are, but last I looked we have rights," John said sternly.

"Not anymore," Kearns smirked cockily.

Katheryn, infuriated, yanked herself free from the agent restraining her and smacked Kearns hard across the face. Her head twisted to the side from the force of the blow. She raised her hand to her stinging cheek and looked at Katheryn with a cold, hard stare as the search teams returned one by one from their search. Kearns fixed her gaze on each one of them as they returned, all with the same report. "Nothing, they're not here."

"Nothing?" asked Kearns, not surprised.

"No ma'am," the agents replied.

Although she did not expect to find them at the house and expected even less cooperation from the parents, she had to ask, "Mrs. Asher, do you know where your son and his friend, what's his name, are?" she looked to Katheryn for an answer. There was none, only a defiant stare. "Do you know where they are going?" Still no reply.

She turned her attention to Debra Kendall, "How about you? Any idea where your daughter's body is?" John stepped up and started to speak, but Kearns stopped him abruptly, "I didn't ask you. I asked her," she barked, her anger building.

Debra Kendall was a quiet, God-fearing woman. She always kept things to herself, but not today. In a rare showing of her inner strength she stepped forward and looked Kearns dead in the eyes. "Mrs. Kearns is it?"

"Miss," she replied.

"That doesn't surprise me a bit," Debra glared. "I understand that it was your people who are responsible for hurting my daughter, and they were acting under your orders, which means you might as well have hurt her yourself. I am not ordinarily a vengeful person, I forgive and forget. That's how I was raised, but if you think for one second that I am going to stand by and watch you hurt our families anymore, you're dead wrong." Katheryn and John looked on with surprise and admiration for Mrs. Kendall as she continued. "Because if you do continue to persecute our families, I promise... I will drop you where you stand like the sack of manure you are."

Kearns' expression was cold and blank as was her reply. "Very nice, thank you. Threatening a federal agent. Kearns' phone rang, it was an agent still on scene at the hospital. She turned away to take the call. Katheryn listened carefully, hoping to hear any hint of what was happening.

"Kearns here."

"Missing, huh?" she said and paused.

"Where was he going?" she asked. "I see."

"You're sure, you've looked everywhere?" she questioned, pausing for the response.

"Well look again," she barked into the phone.

"Keep me posted." She ended the call and turned to Katheryn.

"It looks like we can add kidnapping to the charges. You wouldn't happen to know what happened to agent Tully and his team now would you?"

Katheryn and the Kendall's said nothing.

"That's what I thought." Kearns turned to the agents. "Bag 'em and tag 'em. They're coming with us. It'll be a nice reunion," she ordered with a cynical grin.

Debra stared at her defiantly as she was escorted out of the house, but her angry gaze went unnoticed by Kearns who was busy putting the final pieces of her plot to capture Christian and his friend together in her twisted mind.

On their way out the door Katheryn got a fleeting glimpse up the driveway. "Where's the Camaro? It was there earlier today. I wonder..." she said to herself, smiling at the thought of it.

Hal Porter, Edward Asher's pilot buddy, was working on a Packard built Rolls Royce Merlin 61, V-1650-3 engine that was pulled from a Mustang belonging to a collector friend of his. The Mustang is probably one of the most well-known planes of World War II and the prize of his show collection. He had asked Hal, a fellow enthusiast, to do a rebuild. Hal was meticulous in his work and enjoyed working on old war birds more than anything else.

He was rebuilding the fuel system; in particular, the Twin-choke updraft carburetor with automatic mixture control for the big V-12 when another mechanic walked into the shop to get a volt meter. "Hey Hal, how's it going?"

"Not bad Bobby. How's by you?"

"I'm a little backed up today... you know, every time one of the black jets lands they shut down everything on the field. Never thought I would see them again so soon," he said casually.

"Black jet?" Hal's curiosity kicked in. "When were they here?" he asked.

"They came in a couple of hours ago and left about ten or twenty minutes ago. Looks like they were headed south."

"I didn't see a jet on the field."

"Probably because they pulled in right behind the hangers. Didn't you hear it?" Bobby asked.

"Nah, I've been in and out tracking down a replacement cable for this 'Merlin'," Hal said, playing it off like it was nothing. But inside his mind there was a barrage of questions.

As soon as Bobby left the shop Hal dropped what he was doing and called the Asher home. When no one answered he decided to jump in his car and hurry over to the house. He knew something was up as soon as he heard about the black jet. "What are they up to now?" he thought to himself as he raced out of the airport.

He called his wife, "Hi Arlene, I think somethings up at Ed's so I'm headed over there.

"Be careful," she said continuing, "There's definitely something going on. It's all over the news," she said, expressing her concern. He turned on his radio and continued to speed to Edward's house.

Pulling up to the Asher home, he immediately knew something wasn't right. The front door was open and he could see the jam was broken and splintered. "What the hell is going on now?" he mumbled, hopping out of his car and making his way to the partially open front door. Looking at the door he could see it had been forced in by a battering ram; they always leave their mark. "Kathryn, Ed, you guys here?" he called from the front stoop. He called to them again, his voice echoing through the empty house. He entered the house cautiously, making it through the entrance foyer and calling to them every few seconds. He assumed the worst when no one answered.

He dialed the hospital and reached a mutual friend of his and Dr. Asher's. She had lived next to Hal and his wife for over twenty-five years and worked at the hospital for just as long.

"Hal, is that you?" she asked.

"Yes, is Edward around? Something strange happened at his house."

"Hold on, let me pick you up in the office." She made her way to a private office and picked up the call. "I'm glad you called. Ed was taken out of here a while ago by those agency people. They took him and that agent that got hurt on New Year's Eve."

"They took Edward?"

"Yes," she replied.

"What happened there today? Tell me everything." He listened intently as she explained everything she knew that had transpired from early morning up to the agents racing out of the lot to join the pursuit a short time ago. Then she mentioned, "I think they were looking for Christian."

"I see, so that's why all the commotion. But why Edward?"

"I don't know."

"Thanks for the help. I'll talk to you later." Hal disconnected.

A dreadful feeling came over him as he moved toward the kitchen. He could hear the TV was still on and see curtains by the patio doors rising up and down from the cold winter breeze passing through the broken glass doors. The door jambs were broken and splintered. Pieces of trim torn from the doors littered the floor. "What the hell happened here?" he asked himself with growing concern. He rushed through the house calling out for his friends. He found no one.

Moving back into the kitchen he noticed three partially full coffee cups on the table, still warm to the touch. He then heard something that grabbed his attention. The reporter on the TV mentioned a black helicopter. He watched the replay of the chase, "Damn it!" he said angrily.

"I'll bet those bastards just took her." As he reached to turn off the TV he noticed a little piece of aqua blue rubber sticking out from under a magazine. It was Katheryn's cell phone and it was still recording. "Smart girl," he thought.

He pushed play and listened carefully to the abduction. "This is crazy..." he thought as he hurried out the door dialing his friend at MacArthur. "Hey, it's Hal. Are they there?" he asked referring to the agency. There was a long pause before he received a response.

"Hey Ted, how's it going?" Ryan replied trying to let Hal know that something was going on and he could not speak openly.

"Ted, who the hell is Ted? This is Hal."

"I know, yeah, we had a tremendous turnout all day.

Hal caught on. "Are they still there?"

Ryan continued his ruse, "Oh, yeah... By the way, thanks for the help cleaning up after the party, I appreciate it. I've got to go. I'll give you a call later." The phone went silent.

Hal was curious. "Why were they at MacArthur all day? They're usually in and out. Something wasn't right.

He had just started back to the airport when his phone rang. It was Bobby. "Hey Hal, I thought you'd like to know. They're back."

"What are they doing back there again?"

"They're picking up a few more passengers and you're not going to believe who's with them."

"Who?" Hal asked impatiently.

"It looks like your friend's wife... what's her name?" asked Bobby.

"Katheryn?" Hal questioned.

"Yeah, that's her. They just put her on with two other people, a man and a woman."

"Damn it! You're sure it was her?"

"Positive," Bobby confirmed.

"Thanks Bobby." Hal tossed his phone on the seat and hit the gas.

He turned into the airport just as the jet lifted off, and watched it climb out and bank south. Frustrated, he banged his steering wheel angrily, cursing the agency under his breath.

His phone rang, the ID showing 'ATC,' "Hey, sorry I couldn't talk, they just left." Hal learned from his friend that they followed the same protocol, wiping out any trace that they had been at HTO, and as for the reason they were at MacArthur so long... well, that was obvious now that he learned they were collecting Kathryn and whoever she was with at the house. He was beside himself. "The agency has all of them, but why bother with them? What is their game?" he questioned.

– Eight –
That Sinking Feeling

he nine hundred foot freighter, Olympus, sailed off into the distance having dropped its precious cargo into the cold ocean waters. The effects of the neurotoxic gas that spewed into the container hours earlier started to wear off, but all too late. Christian and CB had recovered some awareness, however fuzzy it was, yet they remained, for the most part, weak and unable to move. They fought to heighten their senses without success as panic set in. The effects of the gas in slowing their neurotransmitters remained strong.

Chilled to the bones, the last trace of daylight visible through the semitransparent roof dimmed as the container slowly sank into the dark water, their hopes of escape fading along with the dimming light as water continued to force air from the container. They accepted their looming demise in the cold dark depths.

The questions they shared remained the same; "Who was doing this to them and why?" As Christian faded he could hear Amy's voice calling to him... he smiled his last smile.

Katheryn and the Kendalls were reunited with Edward, sort of... They were each sequestered to private interrogation rooms where Kearns had begun her systematic questioning of the new arrivals. Her plan was threefold – question them individually first, asking each different questions, then place them in a holding cell together while under observation and monitor their activities and conversations to see what else she could learn. Then, if necessary, question them one by one again using Dr. Crimi's talents to obtain as much information as possible about Christian, his abilities and whereabouts, as well as the whereabouts of Amy's missing body, and if that doesn't work, hold them in custody until Christian and his friend showed up to break them out. A fairly simple plan that would either make or break her career.

Her superiors had given her the go ahead; however, they elected not to involve the Sec Def. for reasons of plausible deniability. The orders were to "Collect as much information on the descendants of the original fourteen as possible, and by any means necessary," and she was prepared to go to 'any means' to get what she wanted.

She loved those words 'by any means necessary'. As far as she was concerned it gave her license to do whatever she wanted, which is exactly what she desired – power and control.

What nobody knew about Pamela Kearns was that when she first started working with her mentor, Dr. Stedwell, her interest in the members and descendants of the original fourteen were benign. She loved what she did and enjoyed the people she was working with from the group. She especially enjoyed the added bonus of being able to be near her husband Jimmy who was a Special Forces commander stationed nearby, but that all changed a few months after the happy couple were married.

One day Jimmy was on a mission to collect data on a reportedly gifted child that had been born somewhere near the Turkish border. This was something he had done many times in the past and had no reason to believe that this would be any different. He and his team were always prepared, but not for what was to come.

When Pamela arrived at work the next day she was pulled to the side by Dr. Stedwell and informed that her husband Jimmy and two of his men were traveling to the child's reported location when their truck struck an IED, an improvised explosive device, and that they were captured and killed by a rebel group led by one Kutsul Bir or, roughly translated, the unholy one. But this was far from the whole truth. This is what Stedwell was allowed to share with her as a superior officer. His superiors had their reasons and his orders stated, 'Nothing more, nothing less."

Devastated, she broke down. Even though she accepted the danger of her husband's position, she would have never thought this could happen on a non-combative assignment.

After the funeral she received a large envelope and opened it up. The message read, I think you should know everything about your husband's murder. Our families deserve to know the truth, no matter what. I am truly sorry, Jimmy was a great guy. It was unsigned and had no return address. She could only assume that it was from one of his team members.

Horrified, she watched the video that was enclosed in the envelope. It was video taken by the rebels that had captured and tortured Jimmy and his team. She watched as they beat and cut him and his team repeatedly while questioning them. They twisted and broke their bones for fun and it showed them laughing as they made Jimmy watch them slice the throat of one of his team members and impale the other after brutally kicking and beating them. But the worst was yet to come.

Kutsul Bir himself walked into view of the camera to warn all foreigners who would dare come to his country that he would do the same to them. Then he ordered her husband's eyelids cut off and made him watch as they set wild dogs on his impaled friend. His last minutes alive were listening to his friend's screams as he was torn apart by wild dogs. And when he was dead, Kutsul Bir pushed Jimmy in with the dogs to suffer the same.

The next day she went to work a changed woman... cold, hard and emotionless, she was determined to find a way to seek her revenge.

Pamela proceeded with her plan of questioning each of the parents, well aware that they wouldn't openly discuss anything with her, but she knew she held the final ace in the hole with Dr. Crimi on site. Her final questions to each; where is Christian and his friend, and where is Amy's body? After receiving little or no information from Edward, Katheryn and John she proceeded to question the meekest of them all, Debra.

Regardless of the fact that Debra stood up for her family back in Long Island, she was profiled as being a generally meek person, and Kearns thought she could break her spirit and get at least some information out of her, but she couldn't have been more wrong. Even after threatening her with the loss of her farm, jail time, and public humiliation, Debra stood her ground, refusing to talk. Kearns pushed her buttons heavily regarding the location of Amy's body, going as far as disconnecting the video and turning off the recording equipment to tell her what despicable things she would do if she did find Amy's body.

Debra just watched, even smiled once at Kearns during the questioning. The only words to leave her mouth were, "It must be hell living inside your diseased head," then a smile of satisfaction, and that was it... not another word.

Of course she feared the threats, a lifetime of building a family and home gone because of some nosey government bitch, but none of that mattered to her. She knew something Kearns did not know, something that her husband John was able to share with her during their transport from the Hampton's to Virginia regarding the call he received just before the agency busted into the house and took them captive. That small bit of knowledge helped her to make her peace. "Screw this diseased bitch," she thought as Kearns continued to probe for information.

Hours later the exhausted group was reunited in another holding cell. Kearns monitored their greeting of each other and the subsequent conversations between them for an hour with nothing to show for it. The agent heading up the surveillance was falling asleep, likening it to the most boring show on television. His head was getting heavier and heavier as he began to lose his battle with boredom. The only one in the room with energy to spare was Kearns, watching and listening intently for any morsel of information that would lead her to Christian and his friend.

Disturbed that she was getting nowhere, she slammed her hands down on the table, waking the nearly comatose agent. "Get me Crimi now!" she demanded. The startled agent looked at her with concerned curiosity. "What are you looking at?" she asked, "I told you to get me Crimi."

His concern was for procedure. Dr. Thomasine Crimi had a reputation for getting things done her own way. It just didn't seem right to use her services on law abiding citizens to gain trivial information. Her talents were best utilized on the likes of terrorists, assassins, drug lords and not, well, not with ordinary people like this.

"What are you waiting for?" Kearns growled. "Go – Now!"

Kearns watched the monitors impatiently for any signs of activity. She had a cynical smile on her face believing that she would soon have the information she desired. The door opened and Dr. Crimi walked in. She was a tall woman with dark hair and dark eyes, and unnatural looking pale skin. Her penchant for the macabre was evidenced by the enjoyment she received applying the unusual techniques she employed to accomplish her job, a job in which she took great satisfaction.

She greeted Kearns and leaned over to look at the surveillance monitor.

"Not my usual subjects. What did you want?" she inquired tapping her blood red nails on the desk.

"They have information I want. Do whatever it is that you do and get it for me," Kearns said, looking back to the surveillance video with a stern and confident look.

Crimi watched the screen for a moment longer. "I think I'll start with the Boy Scout™ on the right," referring to Edward. "Have him brought to me in ten minutes. I'll get whatever he knows for you," Crimi stated with confidence.

Kearns handed the doctor a list of questions she wanted answered. Crimi smiled, appearing almost enthused, "This will give me a chance to test out that new serum I've been working on."

"New serum?" Kearns questioned.

"Yes, it's a botanical extraction I developed and have been testing. It increases the effects of sodium thiopental threefold, but it's been giving me a bit of trouble."

"Trouble?" Kearns looked at Crimi with curiosity.

"Yes, it has a tendency to over inhibit neurotransmitter release, and on occasion it shuts down the respiratory system on smaller test subjects. At least now I'll get see how it affects larger subjects."

"Is it licensed?" asked Kearns showing momentary concern, briefly second guessing her idea to use Crimi's services.

Dr. Crimi noticed her moment and sized her up. "Hmm... not healthy to have a conscious in this line of work."

Kearns took Dr. Crimi's comment personally. It wasn't healthy to show weakness in this line of work. "I don't care what you have to do, get me what I want," she said sternly.

"That's more like it," Crimi said, smiling as she turned and walked away.

Dr. Crimi enjoyed what she did. She was given the opportunity to experiment on the ultimate test subject – humans – and it was sanctioned by the government, at least most of it was. She was paid well for her services and had no plans to climb the ranks. She left Kearns behind and strode down the hall with a smug look on her face thinking, "I love being right," referring to Kearns' momentary weakness.

As Christian's last moments of consciousness faded he felt himself floating toward a vortex of light with thoughts of Amy and the sound of her gentle voice calling to him playing inside his mind. A peaceful look adorned his face.

His transition into the vortex and the next life was slower than he remembered. As the lights became brighter and brighter, images and memories of friends and family raced through his mind. He was walking the borderline between heaven and earth.

In his peaceful moment of surrender he felt the warmth and calm of his heavenly transition. He was once again witnessing the beauty of the other side. There were no words to describe its beauty other than heaven. Friends and family from the past gathered to greet him; he was almost home.

Suddenly his muscles contracted violently as a surge of electricity coursed through his body. His eyes rolled back into his head as another jolt pulled him back further from his peaceful transition. Then another even stronger pulse followed. He felt the chill in his bones once again as the painful aches the icy cold waters had caused minutes earlier returned, causing him to shiver uncontrollably as he was pulled back from the swirling vortex at a dizzying speed.

Christian coughed, clearing the cold salt water from his lungs and throat and he could feel his heart pounding. He was no longer in the water, nor was he between worlds. "But where am I?" he wondered. He began to focus on the strange noises around him. "Where the hell am I?" he thought, trying to get a grip on the situation. He didn't know it, but he was moments away from...

Ouch! What is that?" he yelped, alarmed by a sharp poking and stinging sensation. He could feel something climbing all over him, but he couldn't move to see what it was. "What the hell is that?" Unable to open his eyes he started to panic. His blood pressure spiked, setting off alarms and alerting his unknown attendees who acted quickly to sedate him.

Calm but disoriented, he listened to the clamoring of unusual sounds around him. The muffled sounds were not clear enough to understand. "Who's there? Who's talking? Why can't I see?" he called out, but no one could hear him. He coughed, clearing the final bits of water from his lungs and wondering what fresh hell he had entered.

He opened his eyes slowly to the pain of glaring bright lights, and craned anxiously in an attempt to focus on something moving next to where he lay as a rush of warm air and beams of light began to circulate around him. All he knew was about to change.

"You've got to be kidding..." His focus slowly returned, "What the hell is that?" He lay nervously watching and unable to process what he was witnessing. He was surrounded by a group of unusual beings that appeared to be attending to him, some of which resembled pictures of ancient mermen he had seen as a child. Others appeared to be humanoid and looked like some kind of genetic crossbreeds, and yet others vaguely resembled the sea horses he kept as a child, his Atlanteans, but with shorter snouts and large oval eyes. "Am I out of my mind?" he thought, struggling to get a grip on the situation.

He tried to heighten unsuccessfully. His higher brain functions remained sluggish from the gas as well as the rapid cooling of his neural tissues by the icy waters. His head ached as he regressed to a fleeting moment from minutes earlier and remembered seeing glimpses of mermen pulling him and CB from the metal sarcophagus resting in the depths. "That wasn't a dream?" he questioned excitedly.

A gentle, raspy voice chimed in from behind the group of curious looking attendees, "Oh good, you're awake. You will need to decompress for another minute and then I'll answer all of your questions."

No longer paralyzed from the gas but somehow restrained, Christian struggled to free himself as he called out excitedly, "Why can't I move? Who are you?"

A curious group of the strange looking beings gathered around him. He was just as strange to them as they were to him. One of them waved a scaly hand over the top of him and he felt the capsule decompress. He continued to watch nervously as bands of colored lights passed over his body once again. The attendant then waved his hand again, and the electronic field of glass covering his top half vanished. It felt to him like he was in a coffin half open for viewing. It was the same electrochemical technology he saw on the top of the trailer container, he was sure of it. But how?

"I must be dreaming," he thought, his head pounding from the after-effects of the gas. It was far worse than the experience he had when he was brought to Van Dunne.

"Oh, no my friend, you are most certainly not dreaming," one of his attendants said leaning over to look at him. "Welcome back!"

Christian, both frightened and amazed at the same time, gazed at his attendants. Glancing past them he saw his reflection on the ceiling. He was lying in a cylindrical metallic container, a high tech iron maiden of sorts. "There are no restraints," he thought, "What's holding me down?"

"Now, now..." he heard a voice say calmly. "There's no need to get excited Mr. Asher."

A slew of questions shot from Christian's mouth, "Who are you? How do you know my name, and where am I?" Christian asked demandingly, straining to see the approaching man.

"All of your questions will be answered shortly," he responded and stepped into Christian's view.

"Who the hell are you?" he asked, looking up at the strangest being of them all. The man was like no man he'd ever seen before. He was almost seven feet tall and had bumpy reptilian-like skin. His large, dark eyes sat obliquely in his oversized head. His ears were miniscule, tiny openings behind the eyes and above what appeared to be some type of filter or gills.

"I am 'Noegrus' and as to what I am... I am a 'Seclovian.' I would expect that you, unlike your friend, would have no memory of our kind. Our race is a relatively new one. We are the result of a necessary genetic alteration that was required in order for our species to survive on our planet. Much like what humans are doing to this planet, our technology, wars and industry damaged our planet beyond repair.

Noegrus continued, "To answer your next question, yes... your friend is with us as well. He will be along any minute."

Christian was happy to know CB was with him, but his concern grew hearing the commotion just out of his line of sight.

"Why am I restrained?" Christian asked.

"My apologies, it was only precautionary. You were very excitable when we were reviving you and I did not wish for you to injure yourself. I think that time has passed," Noegrus replied releasing Christian with the wave of his hand.

Christian sat up and looked down to see he was hovering above the floor. "What is this thing?" he asked with peaked curiosity.

"It is a reanimation chamber. We use it to heal some and on rare occasions like this, to bring the deceased back to life."

"You mean I was..."

"Yes, you most certainly were... almost too far gone to bring back." Noegrus appeared to smile.

Christian looked at CB's motionless body. "Is he..."

Noegrus interrupted, "Deceased? No, he's just sedated. He'll be fine..."

"What is this place?" Christian asked.

Noegrus shared with Christian, "You are in one of many subterranean bases established by members of a consortium of planets millennia ago. This one is located roughly two miles beneath your Galapagos Islands. Since the beginning we have studied your planet and all of its species, including humans." He paused, "Our mission has always been one of a scientific nature; to observe and nurture your species, to help you develop. But things are changing now I'm afraid, and I fear for the future."

"Here," he said, injecting Christian, "this should help with the pain in your head." He smiled again. Waving his hand, the high tech iron maiden tilted upright, allowing Christian to step out freely.

Christian didn't know what to do first. He walked around inspecting every aspect of the floating gurney, bending down and standing up over and over to see what made it work. Noegrus then showed him the remainder of the facility. He enjoyed Christian's enthusiastic curiosity as they walked for almost an hour sharing stories and exchanging information. Christian was most amazed with their water manipulation abilities and how they used it to create breathable spaces.

Christian admired Noegrus' remarkable intelligence and was as curious about their presence on this planet as Noegrus was curious about life on dry land. Although he was unsure as to why he was being afforded the chance to see the facility and its incredibly advanced technology first hand, he absorbed all the information he was capable of as they toured the labyrinth of corridors.

Making their way back to the room where it all began, Noegrus ended the conversation with, "I'm sorry that your stay with us has been so short. I was looking forward to exchanging more information with you, but my superiors have demanded you and your friend be sent to them immediately."

"Where are they?" Christian inquired.

Noegrus hurried, standing Christian up against the iron maiden and then reclining it, "Your species has great potential for good. I wish to give you something that may help you avoid the mistakes we have made. Take this..." he said as he injected Christian with a nano-chip behind his left ear.

"Ouch, that hurt." Christian complained.

"You will learn much from it... use it wisely." Noegrus bowed his head.

Christian, rubbing the injection site, thanked him; for what he was unsure, but he was grateful.

"Lay down, I will need to sedate you for your journey. Good luck to you and your friend." He smiled sympathetically and waved his hand over Christian. The metallic tube closed, sealing Christian inside.

"What do you mean, good luck?" he shouted through the electrochemical glass cover. Noegrus waved his hand again and Christian was out cold.

The attendees relieved Noegrus and escorted the cylinders through the underground labyrinth to a transport system. Once loaded the outside doors closed. An attendee entered the coordinates for the delivery and with the wave of his hand a wormhole opened and they were shot through the conveyor system at remarkable speeds, travelling close to fifteen hundred miles in an instant.

Christian opened his eyes slowly. "We're not in Kansas anymore," he thought, finding himself bound to a metal table tilted upright. Surveying the large room he noticed CB, bruised and bloodied, to the left of him. "What the hell is going on now?" he asked himself under his breath, struggling to free himself from his invisible bonds. He surveyed the remainder of the large open room.

Off to the right of him was a series of open-front holding cells containing one or two captives each. Most appeared to be from South America and were talking about Christian and CB as they stared at them with faces pressed up against the bars. The end cell was quite different. It held a man and a woman, a young couple who would later come to be known as Linda and John.

The man was a little banged up but looked alert and strong. They sat quietly arm in arm, observing everything that was happening in the room.

As Christian surveyed the room, a section of the rock wall in front of him disappeared as a door manifested itself through the wall. A tall, thin, shadowy figure appeared. He strode slowly and confidently into the center of the room, looking around at his captives. His dark, unforgiving eyes fixed on Christian. "Good morning. Allow me to introduce myself. I am Adriano..."

Kearns ordered Edward to be removed from the holding cell and brought to Dr. Crimi for interrogation. While thinking about her next moves, the phone on the surveillance console rang. The agent answered and handed her the phone, "It's for you."

She grabbed the phone from the agent, "Kearns here."

"You've made a very big mistake today," said an unknown woman.

Kearns poked the agent, getting his attention and signaled him to trace the call. He complied.

"Who is this? How did you get this number?" Kearns demanded, watching as the agents set up the trace and plugged in to listen in on the call.

"That's not important at the moment. We'll meet soon enough, that I can guarantee," said the mysterious woman.

"What mistake are you talking about?" inquired Kearns.

"Did you happen to lose something today?" the woman asked.

"No, not that I can think of," answered Kearns.

"Are you sure you didn't lose something... like one obnoxious bastard and his two friends?"

"Where are they?" Kearns demanded.

"Let's just say they'll stay fresh for a while. You know, they were very rude and bad tempered. Maybe you should consider teaching them better manners," the woman snickered.

"What do you want?" Kearns asked.

"I think you should know that by now," the woman said pausing, "but I'll give you a little more time to figure that out for yourself."

"And my men?" asked Kearns.

"What about them?" the woman asked.

"Are you going to tell me where they are?" asked Kearns.

"They're not going anywhere," replied the woman.

The agent on the trace gave Kearns the thumbs up. He pointed to the monitor showing her location, a small family restaurant on the water close to the hospital they had left just hours ago.

"Got you bitch," Kearns said to herself with a confident smirk. She signaled the agent to order the mystery woman be picked up by field agents still at the hospital.

Kearns kept her eye on the monitor as she continued the conversation. Stalling for time, she attempted negotiating for the return of her agents. She listened carefully to the background noise, waiting to hear the commotion of the field agents entering the restaurant. Hearing their first command, 'Government Agents. Nobody move,' a cocky Pamela Kearns said, "It looks like I'll be meeting you sooner rather than later." There was a long pause. She could hear the agents getting closer to the mysterious caller's phone.

"Maybe you will... but not today. I'll see you soon Pamela."

"Hello... Hello?" Kearns heard a man's voice on the other end of the phone.

"Who is this?" barked Kearns.

"Menendez, ma'am."

"Where's the woman?" asked Kearns.

"Not here ma'am. She taped two phones together," Menendez answered.

"I want three things," said Kearns demandingly.

"One... answers. Question everyone who may have seen anything and get me any video surveillance. Two... get me every print you can pick up around the area you found the phones, and off the phones themselves. Match the prints to their owners and have them in my office within the hour, and three... get those phones to me within two hours."

"Son of a bitch!" growled Kearns, slamming the phone down in its cradle. While she reviewed the details of the conversation with the mystery woman in her mind, her cell chimed in. An alarmed look crossed her face as she glanced down at the message.

"Nice try!!! Better luck next time... J"

– The End –

ENDING NOTE FROM THE AUTHOR

I'm happy you enjoyed Christian's continuing adventures in the first volume of

Being There Discovery... The Early Years

Please be sure to visit **Amazon.com** to give us your review, and be sure to watch for the continuation of the thrills and excitement in . . .

Being There Discovery... The Dark One

Follow Christian's continued adventures, adventures that lead him to learn the identity of his captor, Adriano, and the discovery of a network of underwater cities and their alien inhabitants. Learn how Pamela Kearns and Dr. Crimi take things one step too far in Pamela's campaign to capture her prize. They say, 'Necessity is the Mother of Invention'; learning he has been betrayed, Christian acquires the Mother of all abilities as his gifts continue to mature to levels far and beyond.

Enter Your Vote... with code 0517

Visit **www.BeingThereDiscovery.com** and place your vote for the question below. Your input will help guide the course of the series moving forward.

Q: What happens to Dr. Crimi's first test subject?

1. The drug introduced into their system results in dramatic, system-wide vasospasm and a resultant stroke for one of her test subjects.

2. Electrodes used during the process of extracting information from her subjects short circuits and knocks Dr. Crimi out cold, ending Pamela's chance to extract the information she wants.

3. One of the test subjects has an unusual tolerance to the serum because of experimentation by the military years earlier and fakes the answers to Pamela Kearns' questions.

4. The subject injects Dr. Crimi with her own serum and learns the inner workings of the agency and how to escape from the facility.

Choose carefully, only one vote per person. The answer with the most votes wins!

Congratulations to John and Linda M. of Haverstraw

**Winners of the *Being There* Series of Interactive Novels
Submit a Chapter/Character Campaign and
the next characters to be immortalized in print!!!**

**Will you be the next character in the Series?
Go to www.BeingThereDiscovery.com
to submit your suggestion today!**

Share this and the contest with friends and family!!!

Imagine you and your friends as characters in the Series....

Suggestions are reviewed on a first-come, first-served basis. If selected, a chapter will be written based on your suggestion, and you will be included as the next character to be immortalized in print!

We have no control over submissions, chapter suggestions or character ideas of similar nature. By placing your vote or submitting a character or chapter suggestion, you agree that you have read and understand the policy, terms and conditions for participation. Policy, terms and conditions are viewable at
www.BeingThereAwakenings.com and
www.BeingThereDiscovery.com

ABOUT THE AUTHOR

R. C. Henningsen is the author of the *Being There* Series of interactive novels. Beginning with the International Best Seller, *Being There Awakenings*. This series of thrilling adventures incorporates a little creative licensing on actual recorded historical events that stimulated the creation of the characters and storyline, the process of which has been millennia in the making. Adventurous since childhood, he rarely missed the opportunity to explore and test the theories of the day. This thirst for knowledge and adventure continues today and is evident in *Being There Awakenings* and the entire series of novels to follow. You will find some of the author's antics and escapades included throughout the series. Other than anonymously supporting numerous causes over the years, one of his passions in life is to provide education and resources to children of lesser circumstances so that they themselves can live fulfilling lives filled with passion, excitement and adventure. He currently resides in New York with his wife when they're home; otherwise, you can find them exploring new destinations and searching for exciting new adventures.

CPSIA information can be obtained
at www.ICGtesting.com
Printed in the USA
BVHW042223010520
579060BV00013B/2976